DEAD BORN

By the same author

Non-Fiction

Lady Policeman

Reluctant Nightingale

The British Policewoman: Her Story

Marlborough Street: The Story of a London Court

Tales from Bow Street

Blue Murder? Policemen Under Suspicion

Dreadful Deeds and Awful Murders: Scotland Yard's First Detectives 1829–1878

Scotland Yard Casebook: The Making of the CID 1865–1935

Fiction

Dead Image

Death in Perspective

Dead Letters

Dead End

Dead Fall

Dead Loss

Dead Centre

DEAD BORN

A DETECTIVE SERGEANT BEST MYSTERY

Joan Lock

First published by Robert Hale 2001
This paperback edition first published by The Mystery Press 2013,
an imprint of

The History Press
The Mill, Brimscombe Port
Stroud, Gloucestershire, GL5 2QG
www.thehistorypress.co.uk

British Library Cataloguing in Publication Data.
A catalogue record for this book is available from the British Library.

ISBN 978 0 7524 6456 5

Typesetting and origination by The History Press
Printed in India.

Chapter One·

He could not make out what the sound was or where it was coming from. It was oddly squeaky, as though some tiny animal was caught in a trap. A mouse? A squirrel? Then, a long intake of breath followed by a pathetic moan made him realize that the noise was, in fact, human. More, that this human was situated directly behind the hedged fence of the next-door garden.

As quietly as possible, he stepped up on to his chair, pushed aside the thick hawthorn and peered over. Despite his care, the tiny, hunched-over figure started and looked up. Tear-filled, hazel eyes met his embarrassed gaze. Either the young girl had heard him or merely sensed she was being watched.

'Sorry,' he murmured, as she turned her head away. 'I just wondered … I mean I didn't know what the sound was … '

She was very young, he realized. No more than twelve or thirteen years old.

'Go away!' she sobbed. 'Leave me alone!' She began choking on her sobs and then to hiccup violently. She couldn't stop.

'Oh dear,' he exclaimed. 'Stay where you are. My Auntie Rose taught me an infallible cure for hiccups.'

He dashed away, soon returning with a glass of water which he struggled to hand over the hedge, getting well scratched by the hawthorn in the process.

The girl heaved herself from the garden seat, swaying as she did so. As she stood up her shawl dropped away and he was startled to see that she was very pregnant. Noticing his surprised gaze she looked down at herself and began sobbing even harder and hiccuping as though she would choke to death.

'Stop that,' he commanded, pushing the glass into her trembling hand. 'Now, take a deep breath and start to drink. Keep drinking – without taking another breath – as much of the water as you can.'

The girl gazed up at him as if he was mad.

'Go on,' he insisted. 'It always works. Deep breath … '

She began.

'Keep going. Keep going,' he cajoled when it seemed she was about to stop. 'Drink it all if you can.'

She managed the lot. Took the glass from her lips, gasped deeply, then waited, looking about her as if a hiccup might sneak up upon her any moment. It didn't.

She stared at him wonderingly, gulped and said, 'Blimey. It do work. Don't it?'

'Never fails,' he agreed, feeling pleased. 'Told you.'

They shared a shy smile. She clearly found this a new experience as hers soon began to waver and she looked down, abashed. Hers was a pleasant, if ordinary, freckled oval face. Her light-brown hair refused to be restrained by its makeshift bootlace Alice band and stuck out defiantly in all directions. But there was something about her eyes which he found beguiling: flecks of gold and hints of latent intelligence.

'Nella!' came a raucous shout from the back of the house. 'Where are you? Lazing about again! I need some 'elp here – now!'

Nella jumped. 'Gotta go,' she said and tried to run back up the garden. Her heavy state caused her to stumble and almost topple over but she saved herself and continued, walking fast.

He looked after her sadly. It could have been his young sister Caterina. He sighed at the cruelty of the world and thought, not for the first time, that this was the oddest job he'd had since joining the Metropolitan Police.

The distraction over, Detective Sergeant Ernest Best resumed his stance before his easel, gazing doubtfully at his attempt on 'loose' representation of the garden greenery. It looked inept to him. 'Do it loosely,' Helen had advised when he wrote to her about his dilemma, 'then you can say it's like the new French impressionism.'

Fortunately, his landlady, after an initial puzzled glance, took little interest in his reasons for spending so much time in her garden. On the whole she was content with her new lodger who was polite, smart and clean and seemed to have no unpleasant habits, indeed was quite a charmer. She merely sniffed a little when he and his easel got in the way as she hung out her washing.

The whole business had started at dawn, three weeks earlier. On Sunday, 4 August 1878, George Thomas Nichols had been driving cattle along Brewery Road heading for the huge, Metropolitan Cattle Market just off the Caledonian Road in Islington. Intended to replace the overcrowded Smithfield, the Metropolitan Market swallowed up a large chunk of Copenhagen Fields one-time tea gardens then a political meeting ground where support had been voiced for the French Revolution and the Tolpuddle Martyrs.

Cries of rebellion were now replaced by the shouts of the drovers, cattle salesmen and buyers striking a bargain; the wheedling yells of boys selling toffee, brandy balls and ash sticks; and the bleating and bellowing of the captive animals.

At least it was quiet now, thought George. His bullocks would not be on show till tomorrow morning. He had time to herd them in the bullock pens and feed and water them before going home for some much-needed rest. Thank goodness he lived in the next street. He was exhausted, as were Tiger and Brawn, his two collies. Bullocks were particularly difficult to keep in check and needed all the goading he could muster for this last lap on their journey from Norfolk.

Just as the Market Tower clock struck five he slowed down to fill his pipe. He knew his charges would become difficult to handle when they turned into the pens and got the whiff of the slaughterhouses by the gate. As he paused to inhale the rich smoke his eye was caught by something lying on the wall at the foot of the market railings – just below an iron pillar sporting a coat of arms and a lamb's head.

He ambled over to give the flannel-wrapped bundle a poke with his cattle prod. Soft, with some harder bits. He shrugged. Some scraps and bones someone intended to take home for their dog but forgot. He unwrapped it nonetheless.

Two days later, at ten minutes past six on a mild but cloudy morning, an ostler named Edward Arthur Jones was walking up the long and dramatically curving sweep of Highbury Crescent – in a much more salubrious part of Islington. Pairs of lofty Italianate villas peered down on to a half-moon of fields – one of the few large green places left after the building frenzy of the last fifty years. Highbury Fields clung on.

The crescent was surprisingly steep (the good air of the heights was one of Islington's major attractions) and Mr Jones was feeling his age this morning. He puffed and slowed down a little. As he did so his eye was drawn to a small bundle resting against one of the fences surrounding the fields. He called this parcel to the attention of a passing constable on his way off duty.

The very next day, about a mile south-west of Highbury Crescent, a boatman spotted a brown paper parcel floating in the Regent's Canal.

Within the next eight days, small parcels were found spread all around the borough. One was discovered in a cesspit, another in a dustbin. Two small boys happened upon a bundle which lay behind a hedge in Laycock's Dairy Farm, and the conductor of the last tram from Moorgate to Archway pulled such a package from the luggage rack as he checked his vehicle before going home. The rose bushes in the gardens of the strangely Gothic Lonsdale Square gave shelter to another, as did a gravestone in St Mary's Churchyard which overlooked busy Upper Street.

Inside each bundle was a newborn baby. Most showed signs of malnutrition, quite a number had injuries to their skulls indicating a violent death.

Chapter Two

'You know what this means?' asked Detective Chief Inspector Arthur Amos Cheadle.

Best knew that he wasn't expected to answer the question so merely looked attentive.

'Another Camberwell,' announced Cheadle. 'That's what it means.'

Best nodded. 'Looks like it, sir.' In fact, the comparison was a bit of an exaggeration. In Camberwell, a few years back, no fewer than sixteen dead babies had been found within a few weeks.

'I wants you ... ' As usual, Cheadle's huge frame had been gradually slipping down his shiny, leather-covered chair and, as usual, he shot himself upright and leaned forward. 'I wants you to go in there,' he said bluntly.

'Take on the case?' said Best. 'Yes, sir.'

'No, I wants you to go in there – undercover. Get lodgings near a suspect house. Do some shadowing. Nose around.'

Best was startled. Cheadle pre-empted him, shaking his head slowly so that his large and luxuriant moustache swayed and quivered hypnotically. 'It's no use getting the divisionals to do it. Too many people knows them.'

'What about Sergeant Relf, sir?'

One time he wouldn't have dared question the orders of Scotland Yard's most astute detective and most ill-educated man. One time he would have suspected this was one of Cheadle's attempts to bring his fastidious and 'arty' sergeant down to earth. But times had changed. The recent disgrace brought on Cheadle's beloved department had simultaneously diminished the spirit of the old warhorse and put Best, proven to be one of the few honest Scotland Yard detectives, in a more favourable position. It had also made promotion to inspector imminent. Or should have done.

'Relf's h'otherwise engaged,' said Cheadle. 'And I wants you' – he heaved himself up again 'to 'elp bring back our good name. Besides,' he added with some venom, 'this is detective work, ain't it? This is murder.'

Well, it might be murder but it had been going on for a long time. Dead, new-born babies were frequently found discarded in small parcels all about this great capital city and had been for many years. It was only when the numbers found in one place became outrageous and the authorities were unable to ignore the situation that it was felt that something should be done about it. They were pressured into action and there was a flurry of activity for a while. Something certainly had been done about 'the Camberwell business' – Mrs Waters, baby-farmer, had been hanged.

On that occasion it had been two local uniformed officers, Sergeant Relf and Constable Tyers, who had taken action and become the heroes of the hour. Soon after, when there was an outbreak in Islington, Relf and Tyers had been put into lodgings in College Street, several doors from the 'suspected house'. They reported 'nothing suspicious happened' due, Relf was certain, to the suspects knowing they were being watched and were being extremely careful since the recent baby-farming convictions – not to mention the subsequent execution.

Later, Relf and Tyers were prominent witnesses before the Parliamentary Select Committee on the Protection of Infant Life which in turn had brought about legislation to see it didn't happen again. But, the laws passed were weak and the problem widespread so, of course, it did.

Scotland Yard detectives had made one or two half-hearted sorties into this arena both before and after the legislation – with little success. Now, however, when the department's stock was so low, they needed to show how much they cared.

Best felt he'd made a good start by actually finding lodgings with Mrs O'Connor, right next door to one of the 'suspect houses'. Mrs O'Connor's standards of cleanliness were adequate but not quite up to those of the fastidious Sergeant Best and he found the dingy decor rather depressing. But his landlady was a cheerful, friendly enough soul – once she had got used to the idea of having a respectable gentleman lodger who was not 'engaged during the day'. Indeed, she had only consented to take him when he had offered more than her 'moderate terms' and promised not to get under her feet.

Her partial-board cooking turned out to be really quite good if a little on the over-substantial side. One would think her lodgers were Irish navvies rather than one thirty-year-old bank clerk, a youthful assistant in a high-class gents' outfitters, and himself – a recuperating invalid with an artistic bent.

Painting watercolours offered Best a legitimate excuse to hang around the garden during the day. Here he could keep an eye on the house next door while, hopefully, making some casual acquaintances among the staff and residents.

But it proved a little difficult to sustain the pretence that the unkempt and overgrown plot, littered with various rusting domestic and garden implements and straddled by washing lines, was a picturesque subject. He thanked heaven for the clumps of Michaelmas daisies run wild by the fence and hung about with sprays of dog roses, though he was coming to the end of the number of times he could attempt to reproduce their riotous abandon in watercolour.

Thank goodness that he had also established that resting in his room was part of his pretended invalid regime. Fortunately the room overlooked the street, so from its window he could watch the comings and goings at the house next door while bringing himself up to date on this baby business – and re-reading Helen's letters for the third and fourth time.

From the start it had struck him how cruel this assignment was for him. Emma had died before they could have children, a miscarriage only hastening her death from the scourge of consumption. Now, he longed to become a father but he longed for Helen even more and children were part of the problem between them. Still, she was coming home from her studies in Paris at last. Only a week and two days to go!

Best stabbed his brush angrily at his painting. He hated all this baby-farming business and despised the heartless women who became involved in it – and he wasn't a man usually given to despising.

'You look ever so cross,' said a voice from the next door garden. 'Won't it come right?'

It was Nella. Bigger than ever, her brown dress now held together with safety pins at strategic points, and carrying a heavy basket of washing. It was hard to despise Nella. He decided to plunge straight in.

'Thinking about children,' he confessed.

'Oh,' said Nella, plonking the basket on the grass and looking ruefully down at herself. 'I don't think about nuffink else, do I?' She smiled wanly. 'Ain't got no choice.'

'Don't you want the baby then?'

'T'aint that. Didn't expect it, did I?' She glanced anxiously back at the house then picked up a pink woollen shawl liberally embroidered with blue flowers. For a moment he thought she was going to fall over but she managed to steady herself and straighten up to pull a peg from the bag stretched around what had once been her waist.

'And you're too young,' nodded Best. 'But once you've got it, I bet you'll be pleased.'

'I'll be glad it's come all right. So will they.' She nodded towards the house then reached down for another shawl.

'Will you be able to look after it?' he enquired casually while mixing pale-rose pink yet again.

She shook her head. 'Oh no. I ain't keepin' it,' she insisted. For a moment she looked sad, then she brightened and smiled. 'It's going to ever such a good 'ome. Rich people. It'll have lots to eat. Lovely clothes and never, ever, 'ave to work.'

'That's nice,' said Best, not daring to raise his eyes from his rose-pink mix now grown too red for his purposes. 'Are you sure that's going to happen?'

She frowned, perplexed. 'Course.'

He wasn't sure how to handle the next question so dithered then eventually just murmured, 'Why's that?' But she had moved too far to hear him when she'd noticed that Martha, the dark and dumpy older girl he'd seen around, was striding down the garden towards her.

Murphy made an incongruous city clerk, thought Best as he watched the man tuck into his lamb chops. He had attempted to constrain his robust frame with a smooth, tight, dark suit but the effort only made his ruddy cheeks look ruddier, his rugged features more rugged and had thrown into prominence his crinkly fair hair and flinty blue eyes. His spare time was more appropriately occupied helping out Patrick, his friend from back home, with his house-clearing activities.

'Lovely chops, Mrs O'Connor,' said young Eddie Linwood. 'You must have a good butcher.'

Always the right word, thought Best, looking up from his supper which was, to his relief, smaller than that of the others on the grounds that he was recuperating and was not, at present, a working man. No wonder Linwood did so well at his job, charming wealthy customers while taking their measurements. The contrast between the sparky, sleek and dapper youth and the stolid Murphy couldn't be more pronounced.

'I certainly have,' said Mrs O'Connor. 'I'm a lucky woman in that respect.' Being Irish, Best realized, gave her some immunity to the seduction of soft words, having been weaned on the crack. But she liked to please her lodgers and appreciated Linwood's effort, particularly since he was an Englishman to whom compliments did not come so easily. 'Kind of you to say so.'

She turned her attention to Best about whom she was clearly still a little curious, despite his efforts to merge into the background. 'Didn't I see you having a word with that poor child, Nella?' she said. 'Be careful there, won't you now?'

'Yes,' said Best nodding casually, then added, 'Why are they working her so hard in her state – and why is she so nervous? I was only passing the time of day.'

'She's over time,' said Mrs O'Connor bluntly as she stacked the plates, 'and they're not getting their money's-worth out of her. That's why. So they're thinking of getting it back in kind – if you'll excuse the expression.' She banged the used cutlery down on top of the dinner plates. 'Kind is one thing they're not. You can be sure of *that*.'

Her gentlemen lodgers were a little taken aback by her unusual vehemence but Linwood soon broke the silence.

'Oh, I meant to mention, Mrs O'Connor,' he said. 'Would you be so kind as to hold my supper for me tommorrow night?'

'To be sure. Swimming again, is it?'

'Yes!' The lad was excited. 'I'm racing in the three hundred yards handicap at the Wenlock Baths.' He turned to Best. 'You should come along, it'll be great sport.'

'I might do that,' he said, 'if I'm feeling up to it.' He'd let it drop to Linwood that he could swim and the lad already saw Best, smartly dressed and with his up-to-date, gleaming, Derby shoes as something of a fellow spirit. This, despite the fact that the detective sergeant had done his best to tone down his natural exuberance to fit in with his invalid and unemployed status.

The conversation drifted on to other matters such as the progress in positioning and raising Cleopatra's Needle beside the Thames.

'I still think it would have been better on the green,' said Mrs O'Connor, referring to one of the first proposed sites on which a mock wooden needle had been tried out. 'Opposite the House of Commons with a bit more space around it – wouldn't it have looked grand?'

There followed vigorous debate about the proposed contents of the two urns to be buried in the obelisk's pedestal. All agreed that Mappin's shilling razor, hairpins and 'sundry items of ladies adornment' were acceptable, given that such vanities were often found in ancient burial sites and were easy to understand. Dr Birch's famous translation of the needle's hieroglyphics, the current newspapers and the assorted Bibles, were also generally deemed to be quite a reasonable idea – always supposing the person who eventually dug them up could read English. But, Linwood thought, the Alexandra feeding bottle and children's toys might prove a great puzzle to future archaeologists and the idea of the inclusion of a *Bradshaw's Railway Guide* caused great hilarity all round.

'Sure, and won't they think it's written in code and contains the secret of how we lived,' laughed Mrs O'Connor. 'There'll be fellas spending the rest of their lives working out what it all means!'

'And as for those photographs,' said Best, enjoying himself. 'Who's to say that these "ladies" are the twelve most beautiful women in Britain?'

'It's all such a nonsense,' agreed Mrs O'Connor.

This was a topic on which Linwood held the most firm views. 'Mrs Penelope Wynslow, she's the best.'

Suddenly Murphy sprang to life, 'Martha next door,' he exclaimed with some heat, 'she's prettier than any of them.' He took a large spoonful of jam roly-poly, thrust it into his mouth then looked around as though challenging anyone to disagree. All were too surprised to do so.

Chapter Three

The lively 'Tritsch-Tratsch Polka' almost, but not quite, drowned out the rattling and clattering of the roller skaters whizzing around the rink – and in some cases stumbling and falling.

Best found himself a ringside seat by a flower-festooned, stone nymph under which he put on his hired patented Plympton skates. As he sat down, young Smith flashed by without so much as a glance in his direction. Best sighed and waited for him to come around again. A skating rink seemed to him a very silly place for a rendezvous, particularly since he was purporting to be an invalid. It was Cheadle's idea he was sure – probably with some vindictive intent.

When Smith's tall, well-set figure approached again, Best launched himself forward, intending to join him and skate alongside whilst exchanging vital information. But he was out of practice so, rather than gliding nonchalantly into place beside the handsome young plain clothes constable, he cannoned straight into him and they both tumbled into a heap. Skaters coming up behind either collided with them and became entangled with their flailing arms and legs, or were forced to execute fancy, looping evasions.

Well, I've made Cheadle happy, Best thought sourly, as he struggled to his feet with the aid of Smith's strong arm.

'So sorry, young man,' he said loudly, as they dusted themselves down. 'Out of practice you know.'

'No, no. My fault, sir,' said John George, 'not looking where I was going.'

Best grinned inwardly and thought, you'll go far, lad. Having had enough of this ridiculous charade he seized the opportunity the débâcle had afforded. 'Let me buy you a drink by way of recompense.'

They found an isolated table close to the palm-fringed podium where the scarlet-coated military band were now blasting out the current rage, 'We Sail the Ocean Blue', the rollicking opening chorus of *HMS Pinafore*. Anyone who could overhear them with that competition would have ears like an elephant.

'There's been three more,' announced Smith, without preamble.

Best nodded and thought, three? 'I read about one in Monday's *Islington Gazette*.'

'Two more found this morning, together. A boy and a girl. On some waste ground beside the House of Detention.'

'Hmm. Slightly further afield this time.' Clerkenwell was just down the road. Despite the depressing news it was good to see the young man. 'How is Betsy?'

Smith smiled contentedly. 'She's very well. Kept busy with the new baby, though.'

'And your mother?'

They both laughed. 'Very well too – and I've got you to thank for that. Saved my bacon.'

'But not your poor mother's.'

'No. No. It's all right. Cheadle makes a good husband. Fusses around her all the time. You wouldn't believe.'

'No, I wouldn't.'

'She's got a girl to do the housework!'

'Incredible. And him so penny-pinching!'

'Not any more.'

They both shook their heads and laughed at the unexpectedness of life.

PC Smith and DCI Cheadle – despite the age difference – had fallen for the same young woman, Mrs Betsy

Minchin, the widow of a murder victim. Smith had won her, but Best, fearful of the consequences for his young protégé, had made sure Cheadle was introduced to Smith's widowed mother. She'd been duly warned that her son's career was in her hands and instructed to mollycoddle their detective chief inspector. Much to their amazement, she'd gone and married the old curmudgeon!

Best took a swig of his ale and said, 'Right. Down to business. As well as the proprietress, Mrs Dawes, there appears to be only two other women living there permanently, both domestics. There's an older one, Mary Jones, and a maid of all work, a younger woman, Martha.' He paused when the band halted between tunes, lowered his voice and went on, 'I've seen several pregnant women come and go, often slimmer than when they arrived but not carrying babies. Hard to say how many are staying there at one time. I've not yet seen anyone leave with a suspect parcel but neither have I heard any babies crying.'

They were both silent for a moment as the portent of this struck home.

'What I need to do, of course, is to catch one of the household with a body and follow them to see it being dumped. Another possibility is that one of the men takes them out.'

'Are there no men living there?'

'No, just callers.' He signalled to the waiter for a refill. 'One arrives regularly with a Gladstone bag. My landlady says he's Dr Helman. A tall man, well-dressed, with dark hair and Dundreary whiskers; he wears black clothes and a topper. If I don't spot one of the women with parcels I'll follow him next time he calls with his bag.'

Smith shook his head in a puzzled manner. 'How do they think they can get away with it?'

'Well, they do, don't they? All the time. That's why they start getting greedy and careless, thinking nothing will ever be done – especially now that Lankester is no longer coroner.' The conscientious Lankester had continually drawn attention to the problem.

Smith grimaced. 'It's a terrible business.'

For a few moments they were silent, contemplating the cutting off of so many lives almost before they had begun. Smith broke it by grinning and nodding towards posters announcing roller-skating handicaps and running challenges. 'Are you staying for the races?'

Best shook his head. 'No, I shall deprive myself of that pleasure. I will even,' he said, dabbing his eyes in mock sorrow, 'forego the spectacle of Mr J. Howe of Westminster walking two miles with a two-gallon stone bottle on his bare head.'

They both laughed. It cheered Best up to see the handsome, cheerful, young Smith who'd learned so much since their first case together, but was still eager and a little naïve.

'The things some people do.'

'Nothing as daft as us,' Best pointed out. 'Now you can please me by doing a couple of circuits and some of your fancy twirls. It'll do this poor invalid's heart the world of good to watch you. Then I shall limp off, sadly unable to join you due to my earlier embarrassing stumble.'

Martha was on the move. What's more, she was carrying a bundle under her arm. Best had spied her departure through that desirable lodging-house facility, 'Venetians'. These blinds, intended to protect lodgers from the gaze of the passing throng conversely helped Best clandestinely to observe them from his first-floor-front observation post – particularly any persons coming in and out of the house next door.

The houses in John Street had no front gardens, only iron railings around the area guarding the stairs down to the basement. Just a few steps from the front door and you were on the pavement. Best had to be quick or Martha would be out of sight before he could reach the street. He grabbed his jacket and hat. He hadn't expected a daytime dash, imagining they'd wait for the cover of darkness. For some reason a darkness drop was what Best had expected.

He bounded down the stairs, caught sight of Mrs O'Connor entering the kitchen, and put on his brakes so as not to alert her. Such haste would seem odd in an invalid and gentleman of leisure like himself. She failed to see him so, trying to combine stealth with the greatest speed, he tiptoed quickly to the front door.

Martha had turned left as she left the house and her squat, black-clad figure was just disappearing into the Liverpool Road. Best sped after her to such effect that he almost cannoned into her as he turned the corner. She was waiting by the kerb for a brewer's dray and one of Laycock Dairy Farm's carts to pass before crossing the road. He held back and to make his hesitation seem natural began reaching absently for his cigarettes.

Just as he got them out, Martha made a sudden dash across the road causing the driver of the Holloway-bound tram to slam on his powerful brakes and rein in his horses abruptly. The upper-deck passengers jerked backwards and forwards like ninepins struck but not quite toppled over. The driver shouted curses.

Why had she done that? Did she realize she was being followed, or was she just in a great hurry?

To keep pace with her, Best was forced to take similar risks with life and limb and the wrath of drivers. By the Rainbow Pub she turned into Barnsbury Street. Best kept as close as he dared. She might know him by sight already and there was no reason he shouldn't be heading for Upper Street, but he wanted to keep sightings of him rare. She might get suspicious if he kept popping up beside her.

Looming on their right were the two sentinel buildings either side of the short street which led into Milner Square:

the neo-classical Barnsbury Chapel run, declared Mrs O'Connor, by a minister whose previous congregation had found him too dictatorial, and the monumental, red-brick Islington Proprietory School. Young men attending here were instructed in 'Latin, Greek, French, German and Hebrew to prepare them for University, Professional or Commercial Life or the taking of Government Competitive Examinations'.

Martha gave these important landmarks not a glance but carried on down past the high, flat-fronted terraced houses and Barnsbury Hall. It was here that Best had once had the bumps on his head felt by a phrenologist, Professor Fowler, who had declared him to be headstrong and passionate – which had made DS Littlechild guffaw loudly.

As she reached bustling Upper Street, Martha turned left yet again. Without a sideways glance and at a pace which would have done credit to a competitor in an Agricultural Hall walking race, she sped past drapers and mercers; boot and shoemaker's; a tobacconist; a tea, wine and beer dealer; a photographer's studio; a jeweller; the splendid, double-fronted edifice of the Church Missionary College and the curious W. Dawe & Sons who somehow managed to combine upholstery, cabinet-making, carpet-dealing and undertaking – all under one roof.

It was a warm and sticky day. Brighter than many they had been experiencing at this end of August, the sun having shown signs of having worn itself out during a sweltering June. Best was out of breath and perspiring. No doubt about it, this invalid life had left him out of condition. Still, catching her doing the deed, depositing a tiny corpse, would be worth any amount of sweat.

The street was now busy with shoppers and clerks, out for their lunchtime breaks. Many were heading for the two exciting, ever-expanding department stores, Roberts, and their up-and-coming rivals, Rackstraws, which stood a little distance from each other in the direction Martha was hurrying. Surely they were not her destination?

Best dodged from left to right trying to keep Martha in sight. Suddenly, a large, swaying man in filthy overalls stopped dead in front of him.

'Gizz a light,' he demanded with a hint of aggression. He waved his pathetically limp cigarette under Best's nose.

To refuse might have caused a fuss and thus more delay and unwanted attention. Desperately, he felt about in his waistcoat for his match case while straining to see past the drunken man and trying not to retch at his stench.

He still had Martha's small, dark figure in distant view when, suddenly, the man grabbed the hand holding his light with such strength and ferocity that Best was forced to wrench it free. He broke into a run, his fleeing figure pursued by blurred, boozy oaths and threats of damnation to come.

Too late. Martha was gone. The pavement had now crowded over and the Angel-bound tram clanged noisily and derisively beside him as though to ram the message home.

Chapter Four

Best sat in the garden unhappily contemplating his abortive pursuit of Martha and wondering whether to tell Cheadle of its failure. No point, he decided, unless another tiny body was found nearby the following day or soon after. In any case, he soothed his dented pride, they couldn't expect him to mount a proper surveillance both here and shadow suspects in the streets all on his own. He needed assistance. Someone else to hand to call on. He would write asking for Smith.

Meanwhile, he consoled himself by re-reading some of Helen's letters which were full of the wonders of the Paris Exhibition as well as doubts about the big manufacturers who seemed to be pushing out individuals. How he would have loved to have been there to see the giant head of the statue of Liberty and some of the art and photography with which Helen was so taken. Then he reached the bit he loved the most: *and so, my dear, I shall be arriving at Victoria Station at 1 p.m. on Tuesday, 3 September and will be very pleased if you can meet me but will understand perfectly if that is not possible.*

Not possible! He had written back to say that he'd be there even if the skies fell on him. He had even managed to extract a promise from Cheadle (via some judicious pressure from the beloved Mrs Cheadle) that, should he still be in situ at John Street on 3 September he could have leave of absence to meet Helen's train. Someone else would keep an eye on the house from midday on. It was now Saturday – only three days to go!

The thought cheered him immensely and he turned to another letter, newly arrived by second post. It was penned in Smith's lalboriously neat hand. One of the talents which had made it possible for the lad to be extracted from the uniformed ranks was the fact that he could write legibly, also spell and use his common sense.

Apparently, another anonymous letter had informed the Yard of a second suspect house. Smith wrote:

They are not sure who is going to keep an eye on it yet but the commissioner is threatening to bring in Relf (he is now available) if we have no luck soon. As you would expect, the chief insp. is getting red in the face about it but Mum bakes him his favourite steak and oyster pie and that quietens him down a bit. She's hoping he might retire soon.

He wants you and me to meet again on Sunday night, at 7 p.m. Then I can explain more. It's to be at Finsbury Working Men's Club, in Rodney Street, on Pentonville-hill. I know somebody who is a member who can get us in as guests, and Cheadle thinks if we get chatting to the men we might find out something more. We'll have to listen to a talk about Northern pitmen first but some of the speakers can be quite jolly. Excuse writing – young Gemma kept me awake last night.
All the best.

>   *Yours sincerely*
>   *John G. Smith*

Best's attention was wrenched away from the re-reading of Smith's letter by the sound of raised voices. They were issuing from the rear of the suspect house. Martha stood looking like a stage gypsy, hands on hips and hair awry glaring up at the tall man who Mrs O'Connor had claimed was Doctor Helman.

Their discussion appeared heated. The man was leaning forward, his right arm raised aggressively and, for a moment, Best feared he was going to strike her. What would he do then? Go to her aid and maybe ruin the case? Suddenly, Martha broke off, grabbed a laundry basket and marched down the garden towards the clothes-line leaving the man staring angrily after her. Best averted his eyes then held up his *Illustrated London News* so as to hide his face as Martha began hanging out the clothes, pegging them with ferocious stabs as she did so. He would have loved to ask her about Nella, having suddenly realized that he hadn't seen her since yesterday morning.

'She'll have had her baby and gone,' said Mrs O'Connor after Best broke his self-imposed rule of not being the one to broach the subject of 'next door' to wonder where Nella could be. 'Wasn't that what she was there for now?'

It was, of course. 'But it's so sudden ... '

'These things are, young man,' she laughed but added more sadly, 'These things are. Poor lamb. I hope she was all right.'

'Couldn't we enquire,' asked Best recklessly, 'in a neighbourly fashion?'

'Oh no!' said Mrs O'Connor sharply. 'That you cannot do!' She pushed some imaginary escapee strands back into her bun. 'That would not be advisable. Not at all. They are a law unto themselves those people. A law unto themselves.'

Her round and kindly face had grown pink to the roots of her snowy hair. Something was chiming with Best. Something she had said. He just couldn't put a finger on it.

A slightly embarrassed silence followed this unusual outburst from their landlady. Surprisingly, it was broken by Murphy, who might well have not even noticed the conversational lull.

'What would we be having for pudding, Mrs O'Connor?' he enquired. Murphy loved his puddings.

She brightened. 'My best apple pie from the first of the crop.'

Even Best's mouth watered at the thought and the sharp, sweet smell now filtering through from the kitchen.

'Oh lovely,' said Linwood, finishing off the last of his hotpot. 'I do enjoy your pies, Mrs O'Connor.' He patted his stomach. 'Good thing I'm not going swimming tonight.'

This gave Best an opportunity to pick up the conversational ball by asking the young man what he thought of the idea being bandied about that the now-derelict site of the old Highbury Barn Pleasure Gardens should be turned into an open-air swimming pool for the ladies.

A spirited exchange on the subject took place presided over by a smiling Mrs O'Connor who liked to see her gentlemen 'getting on'. The pool was generally thought to be a good idea, but it was agreed it was no good trying to make it mixed, due to the fact that when it came to outdoor bathing some men persisted in shamelessly swimming not only minus the appropriate apparel but sometimes with no apparel whatsoever. This put even the surrounding areas of such places out of bounds to the ladies.

'But should they be swimming at all?' asked Murphy abruptly. Having begun to speak he now seemed to be in danger of becoming garrulous.

They all turned to look at him queryingly.

'It's unladylike, wouldn't you say?'

Best had been touched by the frequent reports of accidental drownings in his *Illustrated London News*. These occurred chiefly during the summer months and particularly involved women and children, he informed the gathering. Then he wrung their hearts with one of the latest news items which described how three young ladies, of aristocratic birth, had been rowing on a lake in Somerset when their boat overturned.

'Two were rescued but the third, who was only eighteen, drowned.'

The apple pie was served to murmurs of 'Shame', and 'How pitiful'.

The talk was entitled *THE PITMEN OF NORTHUM-BERLAND AND DURHAM: Their Social Habits and Religious Observances*. The speaker, Mr Armytage, began by assuring his amiable audience of working-men that, contrary to rumour, these pitmen were not morally lax.

'In fact,' he insisted, 'in this respect, their position is far above that of the ordinary working men in large towns.' Oddly, the ordinary working-men present showed no resentment at this possible slight but continued to listen respectfully as Mr Armytage admitted that nonetheless the pitmen's religious observances were 'very primitive' and that parsons did little to rectify this matter. 'The Methodists do much more to help reform these sturdy sons of labour,' he assured them.

Best groaned inwardly and gave a sidelong glance at Smith who pretended to be unaware of his colleague's boredom. Fortunately, after the obligatory religious message (it was Sunday, after all), Mr Armytage lightened the proceedings with various humorous tales. These involved the miners' liking for ale, their tasty shortbreads known as 'Singing Hinnies' and the propensity of wives not to wait as long to remarry after the death of their husbands as would those in polite circles.

Indeed, had not one young widow been obliged to refuse a proposal while leaving the church because she had already accepted another just as they were loading her husband's body on the cart?

He could tell a good tale and Best and Smith soon joined in the hearty laughter.

Smith had been talking to the other members before Best had arrived, so once the speaker was finished, to rapturous applause, they were able to escape out into the club's pleasant garden.

There Smith confessed that he had not learned a great deal about local baby-farming from the men on this occasion. It was hardly a subject to just touch upon out of the blue with strangers, he pointed out, he would return and get around to that. He had, however, received some funny looks when confessing he had a painful ailment and was considering consulting Dr Helman.

'He'd be good for some things, I hear tell,' laughed a sharp-featured man with heavily calloused hands. 'Ladies' ailments!' But warning glances from his pals had caused him to shut up then.

'I expect some of their ladies have made use of his services,' murmured Best.

Best was relieved to hear that Martha's recent outing did not appear to have resulted in a further body being found. Some other news was less welcome. Relf had taken up residence close by – in the other suspect house – and Cheadle was foaming at the mouth in consequence. He wanted results quickly.

'It doesn't help that things are very tricky back at the Yard what with Cheadle and Mr Vincent not getting on.'

Mr Howard Vincent, the new head of the branch, was a barrister, though one with little experience at the bar, also a toff and, worse, a civilian! He had no police experience either but was now trying to shape the old detective branch in the mould of the Sûreté which he considered superior to its British equivalent. Most Englishmen thought the French Police a darn sight too powerful.

'They're saying Vincent would like to get rid of Cheadle but daren't yet. Finds him embarrassing. Too coarse. Not suitable to be part of his grand new plan.'

'He'd be a fool if he did. The man might be ignorant but he and John Shore are the best detectives in town.'

'He's honest too.'

Best grimaced. It was a sore point. The department was still licking the wounds acquired when no less than four of its senior members stood in the dock on criminal charges only a year earlier. The branch's duties had involved some immersion in the corrupt horse-racing world and some had become rather too immersed.

The trouble had begun when a gang of fraudsters made it known in France that, due to his many wins, a certain Mr Montgomery could no longer find bookies to accept his bets. He was looking, therefore, for people to place them for him. They surmised that, seeing just how successful Mr Montgomery was (by sleight of hand), these go-betweens would not be able to resist placing some of their own money. And so it transpired.

One wealthy old lady wanted to bet £10,000 but the villains, seeing an easy mark, pressed her for more. Her lawyer became suspicious and the ultimate result was the arrest and imprisonment of the fraudsters.

Some policemen had been puzzled that, even after being identified, the criminal fugitives had proved so hard to track down. It was almost as if they knew every move the police were about to make. All became clear when the villains revealed that for several years they had been bribing senior detectives at Scotland Yard. These included three of the four chief inspectors, Palmer, Clark and Druscovich.

Best had been particularly sad about the downfall of the bright and natty Druscovich who had been kind to him in his early days. The rise of this officer had been remarkably rapid but then he was able, keen, hardworking and multi-lingual.

Druscovich had been depicted by the Press as the most evil and culpable, probably because he was of Polish descent, Best thought. Drawings of the four accused in dock had shown him leering wickedly, while the Scottish-born Inspector Meiklejohn, appeared relatively innocuous. Led astray by a dastardly foreigner one would imagine. In fact, it was Meiklejohn who had been the instigator. Druscovich had been dragged into it when unable to meet a bill for sixty pounds which he had backed for his brother. Meiklejohn, already wealthy enough through bribes to help his colleague, merely said he knew someone who could be of assistance and who would ask no favours in return.

Clark, the oldest of the accused, had been acquitted and immediately retired, but the other three were found guilty and sentenced to two years' hard labour. That had been a year ago and Best was saddened to learn that Druscovich's health was now failing.

A commission of enquiry recommended many changes including a new name: Criminal Investigation Department; the advent of Howard Vincent and, Best was relieved to see, improvement in the measly expenses and allowances.

The two remaining inspectors had been promoted to chief inspector, and several of the branch's twenty sergeants had begun filling the new requirement for twenty inspectors. Best was not yet one of them and he didn't know why. Maybe his friendship with Druscovich had made him suspect. Two foreigners together. Best's mother had been Italian and his proficiency in the language had helped him become a Yard detective – they had so many extradition cases with which to cope. Ironically, there was now to be a special sub department for such duties and he was not in it – he had been relieved to find. Despite the foreign travel, extradition could be tedious, and Best enjoyed variety.

Now it seemed that Cheadle was being provoked by Howard Vincent's obvious disdain into acting uncharacteristically.

'He's threatening to send in the troops and raid your suspect house,' explained Smith. 'Or of withdrawing you altogether and claiming there is obviously no evidence.'

'That would be stupid!' exclaimed Best. 'They are at it, I know they are. I just can't catch them by myself. If I'm out the back they might be leaving by the front door and who knows what they are doing while I am here now. Tell him

I need help. Ask him if you can come in for a few days. I'll
fix it with Mrs O'Connor – say you're my cousin.'

'I'll try.'

'You'll get a better night's sleep in John Street,' Best
tempted. He'd enjoy a bit of company too, particularly that
of this cheerful young man. He was becoming lonely for
his own kind.

'That's tempting!' Smith laughed.

'He has fixed it for Tuesday, hasn't he?' Best asked,
suddenly anxious.

Smith nodded. 'Oh yes. I'm to be out on the street with
my ice-cream cart all the time you are away.'

Best relaxed. 'Good. Good.' The evening air was
bringing out the scent of the roses. Best gazed around,
smiled, and took a deep breath.

He could see Smith was hesitating. Concerned but still
a little too in awe of him to venture personal questions.
He settled for the innocuous one. 'So, exactly what time is
Helen arriving?'

'One o'clock.'

'You must be getting excited about seeing her again?' he
ventured further.

'Yes.' Best looked away so that Smith would not notice
the tears start into his eyes.

When Emma had died so cruelly such a short a time after
their marriage he had thought he would never love again.
That was before Helen; 'the English mouse' had wormed
her way into his affections despite her obvious resistance to
his Latin charms.

Best had not only inherited his mother's dark good looks
but had been brought up among striking women similarly
blessed and eager to please their men.

Then, while searching for her missing sister, he had
been thrown into the company of this mousy-haired,
independent painter lady who hadn't given a fig whether

she pleased him or not. Not only that, she had refused to marry him saying that to be surrounded by children and tied to household chores would end her life as a painter. She'd seen it happen so many times so, like some others of her kind, she had elected to remain single.

Best had brought his considerable charm to bear and so obviously loved her that she had softened and promised to consider the matter deeply and give him a definite answer when she returned from her further training in Paris.

Since she had been away, his family had placed many an attractive and eager young woman in his path, but all the while he had been worrying that Helen would meet someone else while in France. Someone more of her class and artistically inclined.

But it seemed not. The tone of her letters had filled him with hope – sometimes. At others, when lying awake in the dead of night, he began to hate her and wonder why he was being foolish enough to let his life drift away in this fashion.

Chapter Five

It was twenty-five minutes to ten on the morning of Tuesday, 3 September 1878, and Martha was on the move again. Best was in his room completing his reading of yesterday's edition of the *Islington Gazette*, filling in time until he could leave for Victoria and Helen, when he heard the thump of number seven's front door closing.

He rushed to the window just in time to see Martha turning left again towards Liverpool Road. She was carrying a flannel-wrapped bundle and a small valise. He grabbed his hat and jacket, opened his door and, making no attempt to be discreet, bounded down the stairs past a surprised Daisy, the wispy, young maid-of-all-work.

Up to now Daisy, who came in every day, had only seen this strange invalid creeping cautiously around as if any sudden movement might cause him to fall to pieces but Best was determined not to lose track of Martha this time.

Once again, he caught up with Martha at Liverpool Road. There was no sign of young Smith and his ice-cream cart, but then he wasn't supposed to be on watch until eleven o'clock and that was an hour and a half away.

This time Martha had walked further along to the right as far as the oddly turreted Islington Poor Relief office on the corner of Barnsbury Street and when she crossed the Liverpool Road did so less recklessly than before. She had swopped her usual dreary squashed black hat for an almost girlish, pale-yellow straw, trimmed with a cheeky marguerite which bounced as she walked. That should make her easier to keep track of in a crowd. Indeed, there was a different air about her today – purposeful but lighter somehow.

They were off again. Same route. Down Barnsbury Street towards Upper Street. It was a beautiful morning. Bright, sunny and still yet with a freshness and dewy quality to the atmosphere. A good-to-be-alive day.

Best was looking splendidly dark and handsome. He had treated himself to the cleanest and most careful of shaves and his moustache was perfectly trimmed. The toes of his best, side-sprung, mock-buttoned Balmoral boots glinted in the sunlight, the nap of his chestnut-brown bowler had been brushed silky smooth and he had compromised his quietened-down attire with a waistcoat which, while black, had threads which gleamed oh so discreetly as he moved. He was a poem in brown and black. Not for him the dull, black-only uniform of so many males these days.

Several young ladies turned a speculative eye upon this vision as he strode by, but his mind was fixed anxiously on Helen and their appointment. He had re-lived their meeting so many times. He couldn't forego it now! That would be too much to bear. Still time, still time, he told himself. Martha's probably only going down the road and back again.

Martha turned left into Upper Street. Yes, the same route. That made him feel better. Even though he had lost her last time he knew she had arrived back home soon after he had. He relaxed a little. As before, they passed the draper's, boot and shoemaker's, upholsterers-cum-undertakers, and so on. On they went. Suddenly, just about where he had lost her before, she turned into a shop, one of the smaller, cheaper drapers along this stretch. He, too, stopped, his eye ostensibly caught by their window display of gentlemen's stiff collars cunningly arranged into circular towers.

He saw Martha talking to a small, scrawny, bird-like woman. The flannel bundle was on the counter between them. Martha unrolled it and began holding up several items one after the other. They were mostly baby clothes and shawls. Best remembered that it was heaps of such items on the premises which had helped hang Mrs Waters – their presence poignantly indicating just how many little mites had passed through her hands.

Martha began shaking her head and started to rewrap her parcel. The small woman stayed her hand, pointed to something in the heap. Martha held it up – a brown dress with cheap, torn lace at the neck – just like the one Nella had worn! There was more talking then Martha shrugged and nodded resignedly. Money changed hands.

Martha was leaving. He turned his head away but could see by the window reflection that she was turning left. Best waited a second or two then followed again. He would rather have gone into the shop to have a better look at that dress but there was still the matter of what was in that valise and he daren't lose her again.

She made a quick dash across Upper Street then went straight down Canonbury Lane and on into leafy Canonbury Square with its elegant tall, dark Georgian houses. What on earth was she doing here? Where could she be going? The square, like much of Islington, had begun to go downhill somewhat now that the ever-expanding railways were allowing the better-off easy access to the nearby countryside, but the inhabitants of Canonbury Square remained relatively well-to-do. Maybe she had a servant friend here?

Cutting across the centre of the square was Canonbury Road, the start of an important artery into the City of London. It was here that Martha turned left, then crossed the road and continued northwards towards Highbury Corner.

Ah, this was more like it. Up here there was a plant nursery and higgledy-piggledy groups of small, older village dwellings, undisturbed by rebuilding. He knew they were still there because the *Islington Gazette* reported

that some of the residents were complaining to the Ve
about cabmen washing their vehicles in their small squ
and goats being allowed to run around unrestrained. It
could be that Martha had a relative down there.

Suddenly, she stopped – right alongside the tradesman's
side entrance of the rather grand Northampton Lodge.
Best was taken unawares and had no choice but to keep on
going despite the fact that she seemed too preoccupied to
have noticed him.

Glancing back, he saw that she had made no effort to
gain entrance to the Lodge back gates but was standing
on the edge of the pavement looking north. Then Best,
stopping to light a cigarette, saw her stretch out her hand.
Of course – she'd been waiting for the omnibus!

As its horses clattered past him and came to a halt,
another woman came up behind her. Best ran back to join
them. Drat it. There were only two seats downstairs and
the ladies took those as ladies tended to do. Climbing the
steep ladder was difficult in their long dresses and there was
always the risk of exposing a leg or even underwear. As he
put his foot on the platform the conductor barred his way.

'Sorry mate. Full up.'

Best was aghast. 'Oh, but I *must* get on,' he exclaimed in
the manner of a distraught and fussy gentleman. 'I have to
see my mother who is ill!'

'There'll be another along in a minute,' murmured the
conductor unmoved as he reached for his bell.

'But it might be too late!' Best insisted in a panicky
voice. 'They telegraphed me and … '

The conductor gave him an old-fashioned look, but was
sweetened by the coin which was being tucked discreetly
into his pocket.

'Well, you can stand on the platform – if you hold on
tight and keep out of my way. We don't want to lose our
licence for being overloaded, do we?'

Best stayed there, hanging on as the bus jerked and swayed on down the Canonbury Road to where it metamorphosed into the New North Road. Not a move from Martha.

At the third stop there was an exodus from the top deck and the conductor waved him up there. Best tried to resist, but the man was adamant. Any more fuss and all eyes would have been upon him, so up he went. Fortunately, there was room on the bench facing the pavement where he could keep anxious watch on those alighting. Should Martha be among them, he hoped he would have time to leap up, fling himself down those steep stairs and off – before the omnibus started again or Martha did another of her disappearing tricks.

But she wasn't getting off. Every time they juddered to a halt Best strained to see over the low barrier keeping his eyes skinned for the bobbing Marguerite atop the primrose straw. Once, when they started up without warning he nearly fell over the side and just righted himself in time. He could see by their glances and tut-tutting that he was beginning to irritate his fellow passengers who had probably decided he was at the least eccentric, or worse.

They continued on past Moorfields Eye Hospital, Old Street and on down the City Road. Still no emerging yellow daisy. Could she have alighted with a crowd at some point? Had she realized he was shadowing her and deliberately given him the slip?

He dragged out his watch. It was ten past ten. At this rate he might miss meeting Helen! His heart sank and he felt like crying with frustration. He just didn't know what to do. Should he stay on the bus even if she got off? It would turn westwards at London Bridge towards Westminster. He should still have time to get a cab or another omnibus or tram to Victoria Station if he did that.

Helen's train could even be late. They sometimes were, and that terrible train crash at Sittingbourne might still be causing delays. But if he did jump ship now he would be putting the whole case in jeopardy. More babies' lives could be at risk. This could be an important breakthrough. He knew he should keep on following Martha and meet Helen later. She would understand. Somehow that thought didn't comfort him. He wanted to see her *now*.

When they approached London Wall and Bishopsgate, the streets began to fill with City gents wearing silk toppers and carrying tightly rolled umbrellas.

The arrival at London Bridge was the signal for a mass exodus which took Best completely by surprise. Frantically, he tried to keep watch on all the disembarking passengers as he pushed his way to the top of the stairs and climbed down. Now convinced that he was mentally unstable the other passengers gave way nervously.

There was no sign of Martha anywhere. Not on the omnibus nor among those now joining those alighting from other buses and heading up Swan Lane in a crowd. Best had no choice but to follow the flow.

Just as he became certain that he must have lost Martha altogether and that his self-sacrificing journey had been completely in vain, there she was, joining the queue at the top of the gangway which led down to the old Swan Pier. She was engaged in earnest conversation with a heavy-set man with tightly curled fair hair and a red face. Good grief! Murphy!

Chapter Six

Martha was buying a ticket from the booth of the Woolwich Steam Packet Company. She must be going on that pleasure boat moored alongside! Best was paralysed. What *should* he do? He knew what he should do: he should keep following Martha come what may. But Helen? What about Helen? He *had* to be there to meet her!

Martha was now being swept along by the happy crowd towards the flag-bedecked craft. Best felt an urge to rush up to her and demand to see what was in her bag. Obviously she would dispose of her burden in the waters of the Thames as so many had before and – oh hell! – he had to be there to see her do it. He bunched his fists in frustration. Then, slowly and forlornly, he walked up to the ticket booth and paid out two shillings and sixpence for a return ticket to the *Princess Alice*'s final destination, Sheerness. No use risking booking for any of the intermediate stops such as Greenwich or North Woolwich.

Once on board, Best set about locating Martha. He glanced quickly fore and aft, decided on fore, changed his mind and headed for the back of the the boat. His instinct proved correct. He almost cannoned into the woman but, fortunately, at that moment her attention was fixed firmly on the sturdy figure on the quayside – Murphy.

The throb of the engines increased, the paddles began to thump and swish and the boat sidled out into the river to begin its journey eastwards towards the coast. As it did so Murphy suddenly saw Best and looked puzzled and perplexed. He stared as his simple face became creased in a worried frown. Oh, Lord, Best realized, he thinks I'm after his girl. If he only knew!

In contrast to the solid unbroken blocks on the south side, the tall warehouses on the north bank of the Thames near London Bridge offered glimpses of grander buildings beyond. Peeping over and between were the spire of a Wren church and the monument to the Great Fire of London; in front, a jumble of staiths and pontoons with their criss-crossing wooden supports, cranes which dipped and swung up and down to businesslike ships and barges. Around them scurried lighters, tugs and dinghies.

Much of the riverside scene was grubby and dreary, particularly where the ebb tide had left exposed the muddy, rubbish-filled river bank below the waterline. But Best didn't usually mind. He loved the sheer energy and life of the river. Soon, the grand white edifice of Custom House was gazing down on them enquiringly, then the brooding Tower of London fixed them with its sinister stare.

They were entering the busiest part of the bustling Pool of London. Reefed sails, masts and sprits of sailing ships and blackened funnels of steam vessels all thickened into a forest as the boats lined up to gain entrance to the enclosed docks: St Katherine's, the London and West India. Such seeming chaos. Such excitement. Even the names on the wharves conjured up exotic places: the Baltic, Orient and Morocco.

The sun warmed Best's face, glinted dully off dusty wharf windows and brightly on the crests of ripples thrown out by their paddles. He was almost enjoying himself, having determinedly pushed to the back of his mind the awful disappointment of not meeting Helen. It was almost something of a relief to be free from decision-making for a while and away from the back garden of 9 John Street.

Being a weekday, most of his fellow passengers were women and children, many of the latter running and shrieking with delight, all round the decks and up and down the stairways. He was grateful that the noise they generated was largely drowned out by the steady thump of the paddles and the band which was now enthusiastically striking up a rousing 'Life on the Ocean Wave'. It was a happy scene.

A white-aproned, John George Smith assumed a nonchalant demeanour as he wheeled Alfredo Marroni's colourful ice-cream cart along the west side of Liverpool Road. He brought it to a juddering halt by the end of John Street. From here the doorway of number seven, the suspect house and number nine, Mrs O'Connor's residence, were in view.

Alfredo, who was Best's second cousin, had given Smith some guidance in the art of serving penny and halfpenny licks. But Smith, not being a dextrous young man, had found it difficult to prevent the precious ice-cream missing the small glass receptacles and plopping on to the ground instead. With practice he had improved a little, but would have dearly liked to have another run through himself before he got any customers. But what would he do with the results? He could hardly throw them in the gutter or stand there eating them.

As well as improving his aim, he had to take the money and, at the same time, keep an eye on numbers seven and nine John Street. Particularly difficult, in fact, as the natural stance of the hokey-pokey man would be on the pavement facing his cart and looking out into Liverpool Road – away from John Street. Maybe he should cross to the other side? But then he would risk the traffic blocking his view.

As it happened, business was slow to start with so he was able to stand at one end of the cart without appearing suspicious, keeping an eye out for any movement from number seven or Best leaving number nine. He smiled to himself. Perhaps he would offer the sergeant a penny lick when he walked by.

Being forced into inactivity while passing through an everchanging scene divorced one from reality, Best thought. It was hypnotic. One witnessed activity whilst not part of it, nor was one expected to participate. A restful state of affairs. Best had decided that, at the first opportunity, he would send Cheadle a telegraph explaining the situation, but as he had no idea when that opportunity would occur he gave up thinking about it.

He'd also given up trying to keep a surreptitious eye on Martha while they were on the move, concluding that she was hardly likely to go throwing a valise into the water with all these people watching and if he kept following her around she would spot him and become suspicious. He would merely locate her every now and then.

Suddenly he realized he was ravenously hungry so he found himself a pint of ale and a steak and oyster pie and sat enjoying it and allowing his mind to drift. Drift on to Nella, recalling how he had become so concerned at her wan look that he had considered buying her some eggs and real milk from Laycock's Dairy – but had been unable to work out how he could sneak it to her without arousing suspicion and causing her trouble.

He thought about her dress. She had probably thrown it aside after giving birth, being sick of it and it being no longer wearable. That was the answer. If the one left at the drapers in Upper Street was hers, that is, and he could not be sure. The band switched to a selection from *HMS Pinafore* and a rotund and florid gentleman passenger began to sing along with determined jollity. His baritone voice swelled as he threw himself into one of Buttercup's ditties:

A many years ago,
When I was young and charming,
As some of you may know,
I practised baby-farming.

Several of the more lively looking passengers took up the chanting chorus:

Now this is most alarming!
When she was young and charming,
She practised baby-farming.

When Best had first heard the song in a half-empty theatre on an unpleasantly hot and sticky night three months earlier he had thought that it was hardly a suitable subject for a jolly song. But his misgivings had been tempered by the thought that few people were likely to hear it anyway. The opera was a flop.

Later, however, the weather cooled, the audiences grew and suddenly *HMS Pinafore* had become wildly popular. The songs were now on everyone's lips.

But when he came to think about it, there was baby-farming and baby-farming; some far more lethal than others. Strictly speaking, it only meant looking after babies for payment; in practice, causing some of them to die from neglect, starvation and disease – in some instances, quite deliberately.

There were those who claimed that the Camberwell women were merely ignorant. Nine babies had been found in one room and in such circumstances, some deaths were inevitable through infection and natural causes. Didn't many well-loved and cared-for babies also die? The infant mortality rate was high. Perhaps the hanged Mrs Waters and her imprisoned sister had been merely scapegoats?

Helen had pointed out that if poor women, often servants in households with predatory masters, were not left to cope alone they would not be so desperate to get someone else to look after their babies, leaving them scraping to pay for their care out of their meagre wages, or worse, finding someone to take them off their hands permanently, with all that could entail. If they didn't do something they would be dismissed without references and end up destitute in the workhouse.

The Infant Life Protection Act was supposed to cure the problem allowing, as it did, local authorities to employ inspectors who could prosecute unregistered baby-farmers. In addition, came the amendment to the Bastardy law, with the intention of forcing men to pay for their dirty deeds. But neither solution was working very well. The local authorities were largely inactive and the women had little hope of taking their masters to court to get maintenance and, even if they had the courage to do so, there was scant effort to enforce any order to pay.

In consequence, not only baby-farming but lying-in houses thrived. The latter would, for a lump sum, see a woman through pregnancy, then take charge of the baby – supposedly for adoption by wealthy couples. But, too often, smothering the infant at birth was the solution. Which was probably what was going on at number seven, John Street.

That most unlikely of Italian ice-cream vendors, John George Smith, was doing a brisk trade in halfpenny licks.

His first scoop, for an impatient four-year-old boy wearing a scarlet dress with navy trims, had been gratifyingly successful. The second, for a flower-sprigged little girl, had slipped off the glass at the last minute and fallen on to the cart. In response he had acted the carefree Italian, laughed and shrugged in an appropriately foreign manner and given her a penny lick instead.

After that, it had all been plain sailing. He had mastered the knack and was now flicking his wooden paddle to the manner born. He was even managing the quick squeezes of fruit syrup with a natty twist of the wrist and a little joking aside to the mothers and nursemaids.

Indeed, a small queue had soon formed alongside his gaily painted cart. Taking the money hadn't proved such a problem either as most children delighted in plonking down their sticky halfpennies making change-giving unnecessary.

A little less satisfactory, as anticipated, was the business of keeping an eye on numbers seven and nine John Street. But, by giving rapid glances in that direction every now and then, Smith felt fairly sure that no one had emerged from either dwelling without him seeing them.

He had not, however, seen Best leaving. That worried and perplexed him.

The green, tree-fringed rise of Greenwich Park came as something of a relief after three-quarters of an hour of endless wharves and docks. Crowned by the brick and stone turreted Royal Observatory and framed by the magnificent riverside twin edifices of the Royal Naval College and Hospital, the park made a splendid sight, thought Best proudly. To the right – jolly Greenwich Pier with its many pleasurable diversions and, alongside, the picturesque riverside taverns noted for their delicious whitebait dinners.

At Blackwall, at the top of the loop formed by the Isle of Dogs, they stopped to pick up more pleasure seekers. This place had seen many tears, being the departure point for emigrant ships, but today's passengers were full of good cheer and jolly expectations.

Around another loop where the river broadened and straightened, Best's nose was assailed by a pungent mix of odours from the Silvertown factories which produced or refined sugar, flour, dyes, india-rubber, Peruvian guano, chemicals – and electricity.

Soon, Woolwich came into view. It, too, was backed by green slopes, but where Greenwich had the elegance of a Royal Naval College, Woolwich catered for the business end of war. These substantial buildings belonged to the vast Royal Arsenal and barracks housing thousands of soldiers. Despite the work this provided there was an air of decay and despondency about this once-thriving riverside town. The place had certainly gone downhill since he had last seen it, Best thought, probably due to the closure of the Royal Docks.

The steamer stopped on the opposite bank to decant those people heading for the nearby pleasure gardens and to take on more passengers arriving at North Woolwich by train. Best endeavoured to position himself so as to see whether Martha was among those preparing to leave. Not too near to be seen, but close enough to make a sudden dash if necessary.

And there she was, stepping on to dry land this very minute! Frantically, he pushed through the oncoming throng, no holds barred, flashing his tipstaff and shouting, 'Police!', at the startled young man who was about to pull up the gangway.

Best thundered down the wooden planking and was placing his foot on dry land when the retreating figure turned to wave at someone on board and he saw that she *wasn't* Martha, merely someone as dumpy as her and similarly dressed.

He shot up his hand to stay the confused lad who was again about to retract the gangway. As he climbed back up Best nodded his head thoughtfully as though satisfied with the closer view of the shore and the disembarking passengers that his manic dash had allowed him. He just hoped that Martha had not seen his performance and been alerted.

Just boarded were several smartly uniformed soldiers and their ladies, bent on a day out at the coast. The boat was becoming crowded now. Best propped himself up against the guard rail while he got his breath back and retrieved his dignity. Smith would be *in situ* and wondering where he was. If only he had one of those marvellous Belgian carrier pigeons advertised as being as efficient as the electric telegraph!

The river was widening even more now and changing character as Best relaxed again. Flat, low marshlands stretched for miles from either bank, ensuring that the only large building, the already gigantic and momumental new Beckton Gasworks on the north bank, appeared even more imposing. The largest in Europe, it stood back from the riverside, its line of massive jetties looking like sentries guarding this huge fortress.

A little further on lay the vast edifices of the Barking Creek Sewage Pumping station. The outfall pumping station for all of north London, it had recently been opened by the Prince of Wales to much cheering from the citizens of the capital – grateful that they would no longer have to face the summer stink from their river. The Crossness Sewage Works stood a little further up on the south bank – it drained the whole of south London. Both works had been hailed as the engineering feat of the age. Best had seen pictures of all these magnificent buildings. Now, in reality, they did not disappoint.

With a jolt he realized that, while it had not been Martha alighting at Blackwall, he had not in fact seen her since then! He rushed down into the lower saloon, then up again and pushed his way around the decks twice over. No sign of her. Don't panic, he told himself as he imagined revealing to Cheadle, Williamson and Vincent how he had managed once again to lose his quarry and on such a relatively small boat. She must be in the ladies lavatory he decided, positioning himself to watch the top of the stairs and the deck. But what was she doing there all this time? It came to him in a sickening flash. She could be throwing something out of the porthole window. Oh, God.

Should he demand to be allowed in there?

No, he couldn't do that; it would be going too far. He'd been negligent and would now just have to live with the consequences.

Suddenly, there she was alongside him arriving at the top of the stairs. He averted his startled face and watched her out of the corners of his eyes as she went aft. As he suspected, she now had no valise.

He'd been right! She'd thrown it overboard! Damn! He'd been so sure she wouldn't chance tossing anything that large overboard while there were so many people about that he'd grown careless. The toilet – it was obvious now. But, even if he'd known, he had no woman with him to go in there.

This was all such a mess. He slumped dejectedly, watching Martha as she paused and bent over to speak to a young woman who was holding a small baby. The woman smiled and nodded towards a spot under her seat. Martha reached down and retrieved her valise. Best breathed again. Good job he wasn't really in ill health or he would be considerably worse by now.

Chapter Seven

The river narrowed again as they approached Tilbury Docks where ships waited in line, their masts and funnels thrusting up dramatically against the low Essex skyline. Two sailing ships were anchored midstream and a couple of red-brown Thames barges sailed lazily by as the *Princess Alice* began curving in towards the opposite bank.

She drew alongside the pier of that extraordinary resort, The Rosherville Pleasure Gardens. Judging by the jockeying for position on board, this was the chosen destination of most of the passengers.

Best hadn't been to Rosherville for years but he could still remember his excitement when he had first seen them at the age of nine. Lush and green, they spread along the riverside and up and over the high cliffs which hugged them into a crescent shape. Cliffs which he later discovered had been formed back in the 1830s when the site was a chalk quarry owned by one John Rosher.

That first time, however, the young Best wasn't interested in how they had come to be, they just were – and they were fun. That was all that mattered. He had been excited at the prospect of throwing buns at the fearsome, captive bear who could catch them in its mouth and he had gaped in astonishment at the thousand-year-old Peruvian mummy and the skeleton of the huge whale, said to have been caught just opposite in the Thames. Then there had been the display of mechanical figures to fascinate him – not to mention the pleasurable fear of becoming lost in the maze.

Best made his way towards the centre of the boat. He wasn't expecting Martha to get off here – too many people about. More likely she'd go on, just a short way to Gravesend or maybe even to the terminus, Sheerness, where the spreading Thames estuary finally opened out on to the sea. There, she might find quieter backwaters in which to dispose of unwanted burdens.

Just to be safe, however, his eyes ranged through the expectant crowd assembling near the gangplank. No sign of Martha. He ambled aft to a quieter spot and gazed idly over the side at the hoardings proclaiming,

ROSHERVILLE GARDENS
The Place to Spend a Happy Day!

He smiled at the familiar quote from a burlesque song to which he had many times sung along in music halls. Underneath, the billboards listed the gardens' many attractions:

Constant Change of Programme!
Old Favourites and Fresh Faces
THE GRAND BOTANIC COLLECTION
UNSURPASSED
Dancing all day on the Mammoth Platform,
and Evening in the Baronial Hall
At 3 a Miscellaneous Open-Air Entertainment, FREE
The BIJOU THEATRE at 4 o'clock,
Burlesque, Comedy and Farce
Supported by a powerful Company
Ecological Collection. Baby Bears born in the garden.
Old English Fair, Sports and Pastimes
Miles of lovely walks.

His attention shifted lazily to the now familiar pierside activity – the securing of ropes around bollards and the lowering of the gangway – which was just as well. There, at the very front of the shore-bound crowd, he saw Martha. She was straining forward eagerly scanning the river bank. Her squat figure had previously been shielded from his view by a tall man standing behind her.

When she caught sight of whoever she was looking for, her plain face lit up and she began to wave excitedly. Returning her greeting was a very small, fair-haired boy wearing a pristine white sailor suit. He was now jumping up and down and had to be restrained by a stout and smiling, middle-aged woman.

As she reached the promenade Martha dropped her valise with a thump and held her arms wide. As the running boy collided with her she picked him up and hugged him to her as though he were her whole world. She buried her face in his fair, springy curls which glinted in the sunlight as she spun him round.

The contrast of his sparkling blue eyes and pink and white face with Martha's dark looks, dull-brown eyes and pallid skin was remarkable. Yet they had similar stubby noses, wide mouths, straight eyes and eyebrows which turned down oddly at the ends. Martha was smiling now and the difference this made was striking. No longer a sullen, demonic figure, she appeared warm and motherly. Later, Best was to wish that he had not seen her so humanized in this fashion.

He shadowed the trio at a distance as they walked down Burch Road and through the elegant lodge gates into the gardens. He needn't have worried that they'd notice him, they were oblivious to everything except each other. Once inside, they hesitated before making the inevitable, difficult decision. Should it be to the left ascending to the upper walk, or straight ahead through the gardens? No contest with an adored child in tow: they chose the path which led up to the cliff edge. The boy would want to go to the tower first. He always had.

Today's crowd was rather more sedate than the usual mob of Cockneys who descended on Rosherville on

Bank Holidays, determined to enjoy themselves or bust. It was a weekday and many of the crowd were obviously not oppressed by the need to work nor, consequently, the strong compulsion to loosen their stays when on a jaunt.

As Best climbed, fragments of the various gardens below began to reveal themselves. He tried to recall which was which. Every verdant portion had been duly named: The Botanical Garden, The Pleasure Lawn, The Private Lawn, The Dell with its lake and water birds and, his mother's favourite, The Italian Garden. Down on the Archery Lawn, Best noticed several decorous young ladies drawing their bows – some guided by solicitous males, obviously enjoying the forbidden public intimacy such assistance offered.

The four-storey, redbrick, castellated tower still seemed to teeter precariously on the cliff edge. Outside it, the same old placard offered *A Beautiful View of the River Thames for 1d.*

The older woman, whom Best had already dubbed 'granny', promptly sat down on a nearby bench, took the valise from Martha and waved mother and son away. The pair went off chattering and laughing. Best couldn't decide whether to stay and get into conversation with granny. In the end, he concluded that such a move was too risky so settled instead for keeping his quarry in sight. He knew that up here there was another exit from the gardens and having come this far, he would be furious with himself if he lost Martha now. In any case, it might be fun to see the 'beautiful view' again.

It did not disappoint. Presented like a map the now much widening river spread out to almost merge with the flat Essex shores. In turn, the land mingled with the misty, distant sky. Thames barges and steamships passing below appeared like so many toys. They sent out ripples which touched the river bank then flowed gently back out across the flat expanse in widening arcs.

The whole effect was most peaceful but the little boy was obviously more taken with the view to the right of the sixteenth-century Tilbury Fort. The guns pointing towards them became mere dots at this distance and the full grandeur of the monumental water gate and the fort's hexagonal, moated outline, was lost. But, judging by the youngster's delighted squeals, much of it was being brought into focus for him through the telescope mounted on the tower battlements.

Best had been keeping an eye open for a post office telegraph station. But he was pretty certain there would not be one in the gardens and, if there were, there would be too large a crowd around it for him to get served quickly, despite his official status.

Anyway, post office telegraphs could take such an age to arrive and Cheadle might not be at the Yard to receive it. And, come to that, what would he say? 'Shadowing the maid in Rosherville, she is carrying suspect package. Please assist'? Even if they received it in time they wouldn't know what he was talking about.

Back down on terra firma, a family conference resulted in Martha and child heading straight for the mini Crystal Palace Conservatory, doubtless to view the multi-coloured parrots and cockatoos and to make silly faces at the monkeys, while granny headed for the Tudor-style Baronial Hall. This time, Best decided to stay with her. He chose a table near enough so he could hear their conversation when Martha returned – despite the loud music from the next-door theatre where the orchestra was presently in full flood with a spirited rendition of 'The Rose of Rosherville'.

Sure enough, in due course the pair returned, flushed with the excitement of it all, and joined granny, the boy chattering non-stop as he described what he had seen.

'You're gettin' to be quite the young blazer, my lad,' exclaimed Martha, appraising the boy as she sat down for a plate of shrimps and lettuce. 'So tall, an' 'andsome!'

He preened himself then ran to sit on her knee and hug her. 'You're lookin' after Georgie well, Hannah,' she said over his head to the older woman.

Hannah smiled. 'He's a lovely little fella. Wouldn't be without him.'

Martha looked sad and tried to hide the tears which had sprung into the corners of her eyes by glancing around for the waiter.

Hannah leaned over and patted her hand. 'It'll come right one day, you'll see.'

Martha glanced around some more, then spotting Best, looked puzzled and began to frown.

Best smiled, raised his hat and inclined his head in salute.

She still wasn't sure who he was but nodded back uncertainly.

He was saved by the arrival of the waiter. While they were ordering he took out and became engrossed in a copy of the *Woolwich Gazette*, which he had picked up on the boat. Nonetheless, he managed to witness Martha opening the valise. From it she extracted a toy drum, a plush teddy bear and a navy-blue suit which she held up against the boy. Georgie accepted these gifts with little whoops of joy, which was more than Best felt at this revelation.

After a while Hannah glanced at the banqueting hall clock and said, 'We've still got plenty of time before you catch your boat back.'

Oh well, that settled it. She had emptied that blasted valise, revealing nothing more sinister than a teddy bear and she was unlikely to get up to anything more which might interest him. Merely she'd return home to John Street. No need for him to stay with them; he'd been a bit obvious anyway. He would stroll about, renewing old acquaintanceship with the place.

To say this had been a wasted journey was an understatement. He preferred not to dwell on what else it had meant as regards the disappointment over missing the longed for reunion with Helen. But, he tried to reassure himself, at least he was now on nodding terms with Martha and knew more about her. Maybe that would prove useful. He toyed with the idea of taking the train back to London but he had a return boat ticket and really felt too tired to make the effort to change things now. He would just stick with the boat and relax a little, while awaiting its arrival.

The afternoon remained sunny and quite warm. Reluctantly he decided to forego the maze, just in case it trapped him and he failed to extricate himself in time. Instead, he perused the exotic plants in the conservatory, bought a bottle of *The Rosherville Bouquet* perfume for Helen in the bazaar before descending the zigzagging stairway to the gardens.

Once there, he sauntered through the leafy arbour and shady tunnels which led from secret dell to wide lawns, from formal gardens to rough wilderness. Close up, he noticed, some of the temples, colonnades and fountains were starting to show their age and the busts of the famous lining the Broad Walk were becoming somewhat marred by flaking surfaces and small stains. But he was pleased to see Rosherville remained a very pleasant and imaginative spot. He almost felt happy again there. Small wonder that that clergyman had written a long (and truth to tell, rather awful) poem beginning:

If in London's streets you grill,
All is cool in Rosherville

If in London time stands still,
He wears wings in Rosherville

and so on for no less than twenty tedious couplets …

Best was late. He'd promised to be back by 5 p.m. It was now 5.30 p.m. and there was no sign of him. Smith had served his wares to the returning schoolchildren who were surprised to see him still there and kept asking whether he'd be back the next day. Not if I can help it, he thought.

He was tired from standing in one spot so long and his nose had become sunburned despite his white cap and the cart's shade. Italians must be immune to that, he imagined, unlike fair-skinned Englishmen.

Worse, stocks were getting very low and, in any case, he was starting to feel conspicuous, now that his potential customers had dwindled. Ironically, neither he nor his short-term relief local detective had seen one single person leaving seven or nine John Street, carrying bundles or not.

What should he do? His problem was compounded by the fact that he ought to have told the divisional detective that he had not actually seen Best leave that morning. He could have telegraphed Cheadle or Williamson from Islington police station but Smith had worried that he might get his friend into trouble, should he have slipped away early to meet Helen.

What would Best do, he asked himself as he always did when difficult decisions were to be made.

He should weigh up the pros and cons, that was what he should do. To stay in position might draw attention to himself and this could ruin the operation, particularly since he now had only one flavour of ice-cream left (raspberry) and of that only a few more scoops. But, if he left he might miss some vital exodus of a guilty party.

To fill in a little more time he made a big business of closing down the umbrella shade, putting covers over the cart then nonchalantly sitting down beside it on the pavement to consume the last of his potted tongue sandwiches. He took a well-earned swig from a bottle of beer and lit up a cigarette. He didn't really smoke but had learned from Best that cigarettes could prove useful in moments such as these. Newspapers, too, were often part of Best's shadowing equipment.

Six o'clock came and went. Decision time.

In the event, the matter was settled for him by the arrival of Alfredo Marroni who was in need of his cart to take to the West End to cater for the evening trade. Smith could hardly stay at his post without his reason for being there.

Chapter Eight

This time, Best wasn't going to bother to keep Martha and her wretched valise in view when they stopped at North Woolwich. He knew the bag was empty and was sure where she was going – back to John Street.

He felt an absolute fool. It had been a totally wasted journey. Smith would be wondering what the hell had happened to him and, as for Helen … He'd pushed her to the back of his mind but now she came forward again as she always did. She would understand why he couldn't come, wouldn't she? But it made him unutterably sad that the train-side reunion he had imagined so often had not taken place.

The light was fading as they passed through Erith Reach. A lad began putting a taper to the wicks of the red and green port and starboard warning lights before hoisting a white light on to the masthead. The band was thumping out that rousing patriotic song, 'We don't want to fight but by Jingo if we do!'

The children were less boisterous now, worn out by the day's excitements. Next to him, on a bench aft, a dark-haired little boy lay insensible in his mother's arms, his head thrown back – doubtless dreaming of the dazzling delights of Rosherville. An older child leant against her, nodding off. Her companion, a dapper, middle-aged man with abundant soft brown whiskers, kept a still active toddler named Joseph engaged by pushing a bright red toy train to and fro on the deck and crying, 'Toot toot! Toot toot!' to the child's squeals of delight.

'He's slept most of the day and now chooses to wake up!' the fellow exclaimed when Best lent a hand in engaging the boy's attention by dangling his silver watch and chain and allowing him to grasp and examine it with utmost concentration.

'It wasn't this crowded on the way up,' said Best, making polite conversation. 'Where have all these people come from?'

'The other boats,' the man replied. 'They like to come back on the *Princess* 'cos she keeps better time on the home stretch,' he explained, pulling his overcoat around him. 'Besides,' he smiled, 'the *Alice* is favourite, ain't she? Smarter altogether.'

Despite the boat's superior speed, the journey was now becoming tedious, thought Best, and it was chilly. Perhaps he would get off at North Woolwich and take a train the rest of the way.

He shivered. Had he realized he was going for a jaunt on the river he would have brought his overcoat.

'Think I'll go below,' he said. 'It'll be crowded but at least it'll be a bit warmer.'

The band was receiving some spirited opposition from a large group of middle-aged and elderly ladies on the centre of the foredeck. They were singing 'Onward Christian Soldiers' with great gusto.

Best got up, smiled and nodded at the family group. Even the lively toddler had begun to fade now and the mother's head was also slipping sideways.

He was about to go down the stairs to the lower saloon when he saw Martha, sitting in a lonely niche beside the paddle box. She was leaning forward, her elbows tight into her sides. Her hands were screwed into balls and she was sobbing bitterly. Best hesitated. Then shivered again. He was in need of a hot toddy and the comforts of a warm saloon bar. But he hesitated again, sighed, shrugged, and sat down beside her.

✳

'I could find you a pie tray,' offered Alfredo helpfully. 'Tasty meat and potato.'

'Oh, that's a good idea,' said the worried young constable gratefully. Then he had second thoughts about venturing into this more substantial end of the food business. He might look less suspicious with the tray than just loitering around, but wouldn't it be unusual to be selling such wares in such a spot at such a time?

Doubts about the efficiency of his day-long observations on number seven had also begun to set in. Could he have missed Best leaving and his return? Surely not? But he might have been diverted while reaching for some penny lick glasses as trade became brisk or bending down to hand them to beguiling tots. He liked children and tended to give them his full attention. Could that have been his undoing?

But he had to do something to sort out this dilemma. He decided to act decisively. Best had always told him that you could go anywhere and do anything without worrying about looking suspicious as long as you looked as though you should be doing what you were doing and had a convincing excuse ready if you were challenged.

So now, out of sight of 7 John Street, Smith removed his white apron, his cap and his red neckerchief, put on his black jacket and bowler, combed his fair side-whiskers and stood up to his full impressive height. He looked a different man. 'Your decent, upright and honest look is your best disguise' Best had always teased him. 'That, and the innocent, boyish look in your eye.' So Smith stopped frowning and put on a half smile, rounded the corner into John Street and approached number seven.

'I never realized what was goin' on!' Martha sobbed. 'An' when I did – it was too late!'

When Best had sat down beside her he'd expected he would have to provide explanations for his action. Instead he had instinctively touched her arm and looked sympathetic and everything had come tumbling out unbidden.

'That baby-farming they was singing about on the way up,' she gulped. 'Then those hymns just now! I didn't mean to be bad – I just needed the money for my baby!'

'What is it that's going on?' Best asked quietly.

'They're killing them babies!' she cried.

Her exclamation penetrated over competition from the clunking paddles above her, the jollifications of the nearby band and the joyous, 'Yes, Jesus loves you!' emanating from the Bible class and caused other passengers to glance around sharply.

Best patted her hand soothingly, adopted a sad, rueful half-smile and gave a gentle shake of his head, indicating to onlookers that Martha was drunk. It seemed to be an increasingly common failing in working-class women these days so the other passengers merely shook their heads at this further sign of the continuing degradation of the female sex.

'Just take a deep breath,' he instructed in his most commanding but fatherly fashion. Hailing as he did from a half-Italian family, his English side was more than used to coping with dramatic behaviour. 'Now,' he said quietly but firmly, 'tell me all about it.'

She did. She told him everything.

'Good evening,' said Smith, raising his hat and flashing as wide-open and innocent a smile as he could muster. 'You must be Mrs O'Connor.'

'That, I am,' the lady replied. 'And who might you be?'

'I'm Ernest Best's cousin,' he replied. 'Come up to see the Mohawk Minstrels at the Aggy and just stopping by to say hello. Is he in?'

She shook her head. 'Usually, he would be. But aren't you just out of luck today. He dashed out this morning without so much as an "I'm going then, goodbye", and we haven't seen sight nor sound of him since.'

'That's not like Ernest,' said Smith shaking his head with concern. 'Not a bit like him.'

'I'm glad to hear you say that,' rejoined Mrs O'Connor. 'That's my opinion, too.'

'Is he all right, do you think?' Smith asked, unconsciously adopting the vaguely interrogative Irish manner. 'He's not been at all well, you know.'

'I think he must be better. Don't you? Dashing about like a madman. So maybe it's a good sign, after all.'

'Yes, yes maybe.' Smith smiled warmly. What a nice woman. He was uncertain what to do next and Mrs O'Connor seemed about to close the door.

'Tell him John George called will you?'

'I will. I will.'

The door was almost shut when she hesitated and said, 'Now why don't you call back after you've been to your show? He'll be in for supper, no doubt. He enjoys his food, that one.'

'Well, thank you, Mrs O'Connor. I'll certainly do that if I can.'

The *Princess Alice* was now following the long curve of the Thames northwards as they approached Tripcock Point. Ahead, the surging flares of Beckton Gasworks intermittently lit up the gathering dusk. To the left, over the misty marshes, glimmered the distant lights of Woolwich. A large, Cardiff-bound collier passed to their right followed by a tug going so fast that, Best noticed, the barge it was pulling was lifting out of the water.

As they rounded the Point into Gallions Reach they swung outward towards the north bank to avoid a huge, red-painted powder barge, the *Talbot*, and the row of colliers, moored near the south bank.

The band were rounding off this part of their programme with a jolly polka, 'Good Rhine wine'. There was much hearty singing along and some young ladies were even attempting to dance to the lively tune but finding it difficult to get going on such a crowded deck. One of the laughing dancers was very fair and delicately pretty, reminding Best of Helen's young sister, Matilda. She wore a pink bonnet trimmed with a deeper pink cluster of flowers which kept bouncing as she moved. Best smiled at such high spirits. A couple just beneath the port-side paddle box made no attempt to join in the jollity. They were too busy having a bitter row.

As for Best, he was content. He had his evidence and a splendid witness, providing Martha did not renege on him. Even if she did, matters had moved much further forward and this business would shortly be over. He could return and be with Helen. He smiled as he imagined their long-awaited reunion. It would all come right he felt sure, his natural optimism returning. His day had been worthwhile after all.

The band ceased playing, leaving only the rhythmical pounding of the engines and swish of the paddles to fill the gap. All but one musician had gone below. Only the double bass player was waiting at the top of the stairs until there was room enough for him and his bulky instrument to descend.

Suddenly there was a commotion up front.

'Ease her!' a man's voice was shouting urgently. 'Stop her!' Then, frantically, 'Where are you coming to? Good God! Where are you coming to?'

The steam whistle screeched out a long warning and passengers began to scream.

Best rushed forward where, to his amazement, like a towering cliff hanging above him was a huge, red, ship's hull. Louder and even more frantic yells from many other voices did nothing to stay the large ship's progress.

She smashed straight into the side of the *Princess Alice*, just forward of the starboard paddle box where Best and Martha had been sitting.

The initial impact was oddly soft. 'Like a hand pushing through a bandbox' someone said later. Then, with a terrible crunching and grinding the invading hull met the *Princess Alice*'s engine-room framework.

The crashing and splintering of saloon windows and the smashing of saloon glasses and ornaments was overlaid by the repeated wailing and screeching from the vessels' warning whistles and the dreadful and endless screams of terror from the passengers.

The front of the *Princess Alice* began to tip forward and to the left. Best tried to maintain his balance then tried to run back up towards the paddle box and Martha, but was driven back as a great gush of scalding steam shot out from the engine room with an ominous roar as the water rushed in.

The foredeck was now standing almost upright alongside the invading hull. As Best was propelled downwards past the ship's bow chains he leaped sideways and managed to grab at one of the huge links – just as the *Princess Alice* broke in two beneath him and the screech of her whistle was finally silenced by the rushing water.

The chain links were large and Best's grip precarious. He wedged part of his left foot into the loop, rammed his back into it in a twisted stance then tried to drag in his right leg and the rest of his body.

Suddenly, the big ship shuddered, the chain swung forward and began tipping him downwards towards the grinding, thrashing maelstrom beneath. He clung on for dear life, desperately shoving his wrists and forearms in the links and thrusting his whole body backwards so that it curved into the loop.

The chain stopped swinging and settled back. Best pulled out his arms one by one, leaving pieces of skin behind. He dragged his right leg back on to the chains, got a grip with his feet and, with a last tremendous effort, struggled upwards to where the chain entered the eyehole in the ship's side.

Hands reached down to haul him on board where he lay exhausted. When he managed to drag himself to his feet he stared wide-eyed in horror at the ghastly scene below.

Hundreds of people were in the water, struggling for life. They were packed so close that as they struck out wildly to save themselves they pushed others under.

Some managed to grab the ropes thrown over the side of the vessel and were trying desperately to cling on. Men on the deck attempted to pull the ropes up but they were too heavy and some of the people began to fall off. More clung to a rope ladder but when they began climbing up it gave way under the weight and they were thrown back into the water.

Of the *Princess Alice*, the pleasure steamer that had carried them all, there was no longer sight nor sound. All Best could hear were the heart-rending cries.

'Help!'

'Save me! Save me!'

'My baby! My baby!'

In the background the continuing wail of the big ship's warning whistle echoed like a dirge over the water and the desolate marshes beyond.

Chapter Nine

'Help us!' yelled one of the sailors breathlessly. 'For God's sake help us!'

They were dashing about throwing lifebelts, planks and ladders over the side.

'Anything that will float!' the crewman yelled, as he grabbed a hen coop and tipped out its occupants.

Best found a carpenter's bench, lifted it up and threw it over – trying to aim for one of the gaps now opening up among the bobbing heads, but he closed his eyes as it fell.

'We must get these out,' shouted another crewman, chopping with a hatchet at a lifeboat's lashings and canvas covers. Best turned to help haul an exhausted passenger over the rail and on to the deck from one of the ropes before rushing to assist with the loosening of the chocks holding a dinghy. When it was free they dropped it, too, over the side and he, with two other men, climbed down into it.

As they pushed clear and started to row, they were almost overwhelmed by exhausted and drowning passengers clutching at the oars and trying to drag themselves aboard, some falling back and going straight under – finished by this final effort.

Best leaned over and grasped a woman around the waist when her arms gave out. Instantly, his right shoulder was grabbed by another pair of hands and he began to topple sideways. To save himself he was forced to push the second person – another woman – away. She let go and went under but, too late to regain his balance, Best fell into the filthy, stinking water.

With the aid of one of the other rescuers he managed to drag himself and the first woman into the boat, almost capsizing it in the process. He couldn't believe how hard he found the task. Of the second woman who had pulled him in, there was no longer any sign.

They had now saved seven people and the sides of their small craft were hung with several more who clung on desperately, pulling the dinghy down, dangerously low in the water, until it was almost swamped. There was no choice but to push two of them away so that they could row back with their pathetic cargo. Four more in the water hung on tenaciously. Two of these were pulled aboard one of the small rowing boats which had just reached the scene from nearby moored vessels and the river bank. The third managed to grab on to the floating bench Best had thrown overboard but the fourth's grip broke and, with a last strangled gasp, he slid under the water.

As they bumped against the ship's side, willing hands, now better organized with a ladder, pulled the seven survivors aboard. Best's little crew went back for more from the now rapidly thinning, murky waters.

The other two men busied themselves in the middle of the dinghy while Best, at the prow, grabbed one young woman who was frantically attempting to keep herself afloat by thrashing and paddling. As he did so he spotted a middle-aged woman on the other side, seemingly about to give up. He strained across and managed to grab her as well. As he lay stretched out between the two he thought that at any moment he must be torn apart and was almost relieved when the older woman began slipping out of his grasp due to the slime on her clothes and arms.

'Here, give me one of those,' panted one of the young sailors. Between them they managed to haul both women aboard. They plucked off the man hanging on to the bench and two desperate sodden people still clinging on to the bottom of the ropes which festooned the sides of the vessel that he now knew to be the collier, *Bywell Castle*. Sailors had tried to persuade some to climb up the ropes but few had managed. None who had was a woman: they were too weighed down by their heavy wet skirts and insufficient strength in their arms.

By now they had their full load of seven and water was spilling over the sides.

'For God's sake, save the child!' came a desperate cry.

Best recognized the gentleman he had been talking to as he played with the children. He rowed their overloaded boat the few yards to the man who struggled to lift the bedraggled and almost senseless small boy up to them. With the boy safely aboard, Best turned round but the man had gone.

It was time to retreat again to unload their wildly swaying and tilting craft. A sailing barge picked up the three passengers who had fastened themselves to the dinghy's sides before they began to row towards the Woolwich shore.

Floating on the water around them was a heart-breaking layer of flotsam: shawls, umbrellas, a toy trumpet and a scarlet toy locomotive and many, oh, so many, hats, including a pink bonnet with a deeper pink bunch of sodden flowers drooping over the brim.

The despairing cries of those they were unable to save would remain with Best for the rest of his life. As they rowed away the last cries began to fade and an unearthly silence settled over the river. The only sound came from the direction of the North Woolwich Pleasure Gardens – the distant strains of a gay, Strauss waltz.

Smith was fond of Best. The man had not only given him his chance to become a detective but also, by doing that, to meet the woman he had married. He also looked upon the sergeant as a sort of substitute father, his own being long gone, but at the same time he felt protective towards him.

Smith realized that as the result of the man's volatile foreign ways Best was not always understood and appreciated as much as he should have been. As far as Smith was concerned, the Italian blood did occasionally cause him to behave irrationally by British standards, but it also gave him that liveliness and flair which Smith loved.

Smith also knew how Best felt about Helen. Was that where he was now – with Helen – unable to drag himself away? Had he thrown caution to the winds? Taken a chance he wouldn't be found out? It was possible. He didn't know, of course, that Smith had been instructed to report back to Cheadle that very evening when the Cheadles would be coming for supper.

Much as he would like to, he saw no way that he could cover his sergeant's tracks. In any case, Best could be in danger and hiding the fact from his superiors could make things worse.

But what should he do now? It was a problem. To leave it and go back to John Street later would not be a good idea, he decided. Best had once told him that sometimes it is better to take some action, even if it turns out to be wrong. That was preferable than just letting things slide – not knowing what was going on – losing control of the situation. Smith was not sure he agreed but he took a deep breath and made another firm decision.

The ancient town of Woolwich had seen more than its fair share of tragedies since it had first risen to prominence when Henry VIII established the Royal Dockyard in 1512. Many famous ships had been built there including the Great Harry, the flagship of Henry's new Royal Navy. But most of Woolwich's recent disasters were connected with the Royal Arsenal and so had always been well heralded. Heard before being identified.

In 1845, there was an explosion in a laboratory where fuses were being dismantled – killing seven workers. Ten years on, four more men were unceremoniously sent to meet their Maker by an explosion in the rocket shed.

Few of Woolwich's catalogue of catastrophies was quite so well broadcast as that of 1856. Brought about by haste in the preparations for celebrations marking the end of the Crimean War, a rocket ignited, setting off 20,000 squibs and a number of starlight fireworks. The result was a spectacular firework display, one death and many injuries. Eleven days later two men died in an accident in the percussion cap shed.

Worse was to come in 1867 when twenty-four young lads were badly burned while making blank cartridges for the new, breech-loading, Snider rifle. Five of them later died. The following year three men were badly injured when disposing of some fulminate of mercury, seized from a Hamburg-bound vessel. One of them, a police inspector, eventually died of his injuries.

During the oh-so-secret 1874 trials of the fish torpedo (designed to wreak havoc on enemy ships) a man was blown to pieces and several others injured.

It appeared that every material used in the production of armaments was capable of killing of its own volition. All except gun cotton – a material produced by soaking cotton with sulphuric and nitric acid – but which, the workers were assured, was harmless unless deliberately detonated.

The gun cotton explosion took place on 24 May 1875, when, in the cause of experiment, two workers were packing the cotton into a shell with the aid of a hydraulic press. Both died when it self-detonated.

Thus Woolwich was well prepared for noisy tragedies often followed or accompanied by dazzling skies. But when the greatest tragedy ever to occur in their vicinity or, come to that, in the whole of the British Isles, took place, it stole in on slippered feet and caught them unawares.

The first inkling that anything at all untoward had taken place just off their river bank had been the prolonged and mournful wail of the ships' warning sirens drifting in over the marshes on the peaceful evening air. But one of them had soon ceased its bleating and the other faded shortly afterwards. The people of Woolwich were also well accustomed to warning river noises which came and went, generally without consequence.

So, it wasn't until pier hands heard an anguished hail from an approaching rowing-boat and a clearly distressed waterman had jumped on to their floating platform that they realized something dreadful was amiss. Huddled in the small boat were five saturated and shivering adults and one child. Laid out on the bottom were four bodies.

Helen was surprised to see the handsome young police officer.

'John George,' she smiled. 'How nice to see you. Come in.'

Smith had not yet mastered completely the art of hiding his feelings, despite Best's insistence that this was a part of a policeman's armour. He smiled and nodded but at the same time blurted out, 'Is he here?'

'Is who here?' She stood aside to allow him entry. 'Do you mean Ernest?'

'Yes?'

'Ah. I would have thought you would know that better than I since he did not meet me at the station as promised.'

'He didn't!' Smith was shocked.

'No.' She indicated a fireside chair but Smith was too agitated to sit down. 'I assumed something had come up with regard to his work.'

'No. Well, yes. It must have done.' He sat down heavily.

'Take a deep breath and tell me all about it,' said Helen soothingly.

So it was a boating accident. Woolwich had had a few of those as well. Only five years earlier, nine workmen had drowned when their boat capsized while they tried desperately to get across to work in Silvertown despite impenetrable fog.

But the waterman was babbling about the *Princess Alice* – which they knew was now three quarters of an hour overdue – and talking about hundreds of people drowning. The knot of workmen who had gathered around the sodden survivors soon became a small crowd and word rapidly spread.

The survivors, wrapped in blankets, were soon huddling around the fire in the kitchen of the Steam Packet public house while the four bodies were placed in an outhouse of the Ship and Half Moon Inn. In the slum-ridden streets by the pier, 'the dusthole' as it was called, larger crowds were gathering. It couldn't be true. Hundreds of people? Where were they all then?

When Best's dinghy arrived a dozen hands reached out to help him and the little boy out of the boat. The people hereabouts were poor but they desperately wanted to help. A woman tried to take the little boy away to look after him but he screamed and clung to Best's soaked and slimy legs.

'Come with me, both of you,' commanded a middle-aged man with a kindly face. 'I'll get you some dry clothes and a warm fire.'

Helen waited around the corner in the Liverpool Road while Smith knocked once again on Mrs O'Connor's door.

'Wasn't that a short programme then?' she exclaimed on seeing him.

Smith grinned ruefully. 'I'd mistaken the evening,' he confided. 'The house was nearly full so I decided, instead of sitting in a bad seat, I'd rather come and have a chat with good old cousin Ernie.'

'Ah, now, haven't I got to disappoint you there.' She shook her head. 'The man's not back yet.'

'Oh!' Smith was really worried now. Had the next-door neighbours suspected something and done something terrible to Best?

'Don't look so worried, young man,' the amiable landlady cajoled him. 'Sure, it's unlike the gentleman in question but don't we all do something unlike ourselves sometimes?' She smiled. 'As a matter of fact he's gone on a jolly day out on the river.'

The news startled Smith even more but this time he managed to hide his perplexity with a grin. 'Has he now? The old devil.'

'Yes. The only reason I know this is one of my other gentlemen actually saw him boarding the *Princess Alice* pleasure steamer at London Bridge this morning. The boat was bound for Sheerness but who's to know how far he was planning to go?'

'Well, I'm sure the air will do him the world of good,' he assured Mrs O'Connor nonchalantly. 'I'm only sorry I've missed him.'

Smith was now even more puzzled but realized that his sergeant would have a good reason for doing what Mrs O'Connor referred to as 'unlike the gentleman in question'.

Very likely he was shadowing a suspect. That must be it. Best was following someone and had had no time to either send a messenger or a telegram to the Yard. Or then again, maybe he had, and no one had bothered to let Smith know. That would be typical, wouldn't it?

Chapter Ten

The portly, middle-aged man was growing breathless *Wether ?* as he hurried his charges down Bell Water Gate and into Woolwich High Street, a place of many taverns. He halted before a shop which proclaimed itself as George Robertson, Gentleman's Outfitters', pulled out some keys and unlocked the big glass door. He shepherded them through the shop into a small room where a tiny lady sat darning socks before a black-leaded kitchen range. Her eyes widened at the sight of them.

'A terrible accident, Hilda my dear. Down on the river.' The mantelpiece clock began to chime sweetly. The woman held out her arms to the drenched and bedraggled Joseph, exclaiming, 'Oh you poor little thing.'

This sudden thrust into warm, clean and welcoming surroundings disorientated Best almost as much as the accident.

'Sit down. Sit down,' said Hilda, pulling a chair towards the fire.

Best, suddenly aware of his filthy, stinking state looked helplessly down at himself and shook his head.

The couple glanced at each other then, unceremoniously, began to strip the pair down before wrapping them in old blankets. George filled two huge iron pans with water, settled them over the coals and topped up the kettle which had been resting on the hob.

'We'll get you washed and warm in a trice,' said Hilda firmly.

Best felt as if he and Joseph were small boys who'd fallen into a pond when told not to play on the ice, and now needed their mummy. He certainly did, but Joseph seemed too dazed to react.

Soon the pair were washed, patted and rubbed dry, wrapped in clean blankets and sat by the fire with mugs of hot soup in their hands. As soon as he sat down Joseph's eyes had begun to close. Now his head fell forward as sleep claimed him.

George caught the tilting mug and gathered him up, saying, 'I think we'll have to wait until morning before we find a suit for Joseph.'

'I have to ... I have to ... ' Best was having difficulty getting his words out. 'I must ... '

Hilda patted his arm. 'Look for his mother, of course.'

'I'll get you some clothes,' said George, 'while Hilda puts Joseph to bed.'

The shop clearly provided only for the poorer men of Woolwich. But, for once, Best cared little about what he would look like after George had finished quickly and expertly taking his measurements. Oddly, it was now that he was safe, warm and dressed again in dry clothes that he began to shiver and shake.

'I must go back to the pier,' he said.

Smith and Helen only just managed to scramble on board the omnibus. Downstairs was so packed that they had to endure the swaying climb up the almost vertical stairs to the top deck, Smith going up first to save Helen from the possibility of embarrassment.

He knew why some men favoured the top deck – the possible delights to be enjoyed while getting there. But the sight of ladies' underwear was no temptation to Smith. He had seen so much of it strung out to dry in their kitchen when his widowed mother took in washing. Such garments did, however, hold a proud place in his heart. His expertise in the subject had helped identify a murder victim and so enabled him to become a detective.

He turned to assist Helen up the last steps but she seemed to be managing with ease, aided no doubt by the lightness of her strangely narrow dress which hung in limp folds, seemingly lacking support from bustle, petticoats or even corset. Extraordinary.

Her underwear, he acknowledged, would be a complete mystery to him. Maybe she was wearing the latest style from Paris. What, he wondered, would a sharp and natty dresser like Best make of such shapeless, unflattering attire?

Come to that, it had always been a complete mystery to him how such an ordinary-looking woman, with her neat but unexceptional features, mousy-brown little bun and quiet voice could hold such fascination for his vibrant and attractive sergeant. Best, Smith was sure, could have almost any woman he wanted.

Smith was obliged to use his strong shoulders and a little insistence to make enough space for both of them on the benches but the tight packing did help keep him warm. It was a pleasant moonlit night but a distinct chill was creeping into the air and Smith was still lightly clad as for a sunny day selling ice-cream.

Helen turned her head and looked up at him enquiringly. 'Does it not seem strange, John George,' she said, in that disconcertingly direct manner of hers, 'that so many people are coming in this direction at this time of night?'

'Yes. I was thinking that,' the young man nodded. 'Can't be that many people living by London Bridge.' He shrugged. 'But this is one of the last omnibuses. Maybe they'll all be getting off down the New North Road.'

But they didn't. Indeed, many more people tried to get on board there but were repelled by the conductor. Where were they all going?

'They could be changing on to East End omnibuses further down,' he said.

Helen nodded. She wasn't a woman given to unnecessary talk so Smith fell to wondering what his wife would be thinking right now. He'd been sure he'd be back for supper. The arrangement with Best had been so cut and dried. And it was going to be hotpot tonight. He sighed. What they were doing now was just ridiculous.

Helen had insisted that they go down to the Old Swan Pier to meet Best. True, he should have been back by now. They had waited for over an hour within sight of John Street for his return. Smith guessed that the boat's arrival had been delayed for some reason, or Best had had difficulty getting on the packed omnibuses leaving London Bridge and they could even have been held up in traffic after that. They'd probably passed him going the other way. He would be back at John Street now, enjoying the supper Mrs O'Connor was keeping hot for him, Smith thought crossly.

Then again, he might have left the *Princess Alice* further down the river when in pursuit of whoever he was in pursuit of ... oh, this was all too silly. But Helen was not a woman to be balked, at least not by him, and he had asked for her help.

'There's an Archway-bound omnibus coming,' he said touching her arm. 'You look at the upper deck to see if he's there and I'll try below.'

But there proved to be very few passengers going in the other direction. A lone, top-hatted, male smoking a fat cigar sat on the bench facing them on the upper deck but Smith's view into the lower deck was impeded not only by the low slung slats announcing the bus route: Westminster, London Bridge, Holloway Road, Archway Tavern, but also by the vehicle's interior oil lamp as it bumped and swayed along.

He could just make out one female and two male figures, neither of whom seemed like Best, but he couldn't be sure of that. In any case, Best could be sitting on the other side out of his sight altogether – which just showed how ridiculous this whole business was. The hotpot would be all gone by now and he was very hungry.

The creaking and rattling of the other bus grew fainter. They were left with just the heavy plodding of their own pair of horses and the trundle of their own wheels occasionally counterpointed by the livelier clip-clopping trot of a passing hansom cab.

The whole population of Woolwich seemed to be gathered in the streets leading to the waterside, but all that was being brought in now were bodies, and not many of those.

To the forefront of the crowds outside the Woolwich Steamship Company's offices at Roff's Wharf, was W.T. Vincent, solid citizen of Woolwich and chief reporter of the *Kentish Independent*.

W.T. was later to enquire:

> When the Furies planned this dire misfortune why should they have laid the scene at Woolwich? Were we not sufficiently notorious for deeds of evil – murders, explosions, fires, floods, fogs, wrecks, and riots, not to speak of a reputation founded and established on the fiendish trade of war?

And, indeed it was true about the murders and riots, as well as fires and explosions. These were largely due to the great numbers of bored and restless young men garrisoned thereabouts. Young men with easy access to drink, swords and firearms.

All of which had given the slight, bespectacled and unprepossessing Vincent remarkable experience in acting quickly and decisively in getting his news and broadcasting it to the world. Now, having warned the telegraph clerks at the post office to expect a long dispatch to *The Times* he was quickly culling material to fill it from the police, boatmen, survivors and onlookers. He homed in on Best who, in turn, soon realized that this man was the fount of information hereabouts and stuck with him.

Best had decided not to announce himself to the police until his self-appointed tasks were done. He recognized some of them, particularly the inspector in charge, Phillips, but they were too overwhelmed by duty to spot him among the excited milling crowds.

Ironically, the first bodies were taken to the boardroom of the Woolwich Steamship Company. Even more sadly ironic, Best learned, was that one of the first to be laid down there with an identity label tied to her blouse was Mrs Towse, wife of the superintendent of the steamship fleet.

She had gone aboard the *Princess Alice* but a few hours earlier with their six children – none of whom had so far been found. Mr Towse was obliged to carry on, organizing matters on behalf of his company and the passengers, alive and dead. Soon the gas was lit in the Town Hall and space prepared for more bodies.

'Where are all the survivors?' Best asked.

Vincent hesitated, then said quietly, 'There don't seem to be that many.'

Best shook his head. 'But there were hundreds on board and we saved … ' How many had they saved? A handful. Only a handful and hadn't he seen all those poor wretches drowning? But, surely, many more must have been saved. He felt confused. 'I expect most of them were taken over to the other bank. That's it.'

'Yes. Some,' Vincent nodded. 'I know there are some over there.' He rubbed his short, bristly beard. He had a lot more work to do. 'Look,' he said kindly, 'there are a few in the Steam Packet public house.' He glanced at his notes. 'Yes. One of them is called Martha. Martha Barrow. Is that your lady friend?'

'Best shrugged. 'I don't know her second name. I'll have to go and look.'

'Better hurry. I've heard they're moving them on to the infirmary soon.'

None of the other passengers alighted down the New
North Road. Nor at points further south. Indeed, there was
no movement at all until the omnibus arrived at London
Bridge when there was a dash for the exit. Once off the
'bus, nearly all the passengers began rushing down Swan
Lane towards the Old Swan Pier. Numbers were swelled
by passengers spilling out of omnibuses and trams from the
East End, Westminster and south of the river.

Smith and Helen joined the moving throng. The speed
increased as an atmosphere of apprehension took hold.
Looking about them, registering how many others were
on a similar errand, people began to suspect that something
must be wrong. Very wrong.

'They could have been held up by late boarding,' Helen
panted breathlessly, as she strove to keep pace with those
around her.

'Or some mechanical failure,' agreed Smith.

'It's not like the railway.'

She was right. Terrible accidents seemed to be daily
occurrences on the railways and even those were rarely
as bad as first reported. In comparison, river accidents
were few and much less serious. This was all a fuss about
nothing. Crowd mania.

As they reached the pier, Smith realized that most of
those tramping down the gangway and on to the wooden
jetty were men. Not surprising, really. It was a weekday
and these men would have been at work whilst their wives,
children and grandparents took the opportunity to enjoy a
fine, late-summer day out.

The lamp was still glowing over the doorway of the
London Steamboat Company's ticket booth, but the
quayside remained empty. There was no sign of the *Princess
Alice*.

There seemed to be a commotion near the booth.
Voices were raised and hands thrown in the air. There was

shouting and crying out. Those at the back began pushing forward to find out what was happening.

'What's going on!' exclaimed an elderly man with a blotchy red face and rheumy eyes. 'What's happened?'

'Just what I want to know,' said Smith. But nobody was listening.

In an instant, those at the front of the crowd turned as one and began to rush straight towards those still approaching. At first it seemed as if there might be injury or even loss of life in the ensuing mêlée. But the rear of the crowd parted to let them through, shouting questions at the frantic looking people pushing past them.

'Accident,' was the word which Smith caught. Then louder. 'There's been an accident!'

But where were they all going?

An obese, middle-aged woman wearing a black silk bombazine dress and using her umbrella as a battering ram was holding her handkerchief to her mouth and exclaiming, 'Oh, no! Oh, no!' But her girth slowed her down. Smith managed to grab her arm and yelled, 'Where are you all going?'

'To the steamboat offices,' she panted. 'Off Cheapside.'

'They don't know nuffink here,' put in a weedy little man indicating the ticket booth with his backwardly extended thumb. 'Nuffink at all. Just a h'accident, they says. No more information.'

Smith sighed. All this panic before they even knew anything! It was probably nothing more than a bump which had damaged the paddles. But, since it was too late for his hotpot they might as well join the march heading north-west through the city to Cheapside.

'How far do you think it is?' panted Helen as she tried to keep up with John George's long strides.

'I don't know. A half-mile, maybe more.'

She shook her head at the surrounding throng. 'It's going to be chaos when we get there.'

'Don't worry, I'll get through showing my police identity.'

He grabbed her sleeve to prevent her stepping into the path of an empty hawker's cart galloping along Upper Thames Street. 'Be careful! Sergeant Best will kill me if anything happens to you,'

He realized instantly he'd said the wrong thing. It wasn't just the street lighting that had drained her face of colour.

'You don't think anything has happened to him, do you?' she whispered.

'No! Not Best. This is all a fuss about nothing, you'll see.' He guided her between a too-leisurely brougham and a fourwheeler cab loaded with luggage, dashing for the nearby railway station.

He could see she was not comforted.

'Best can swim,' he said stopping abruptly to face her. 'He told me so when we were on the canal case. And, anyway, if there has been an accident, why should it be him out of hundreds … ?'

He had always thought her a rather unemotional woman but now she was gripping his wrist with such ferocity that it hurt.

'But we don't really know, do we?' she said, taking a deep breath and clearly trying to quell rising fear.

'No, we don't,' he admitted finally.

This seemed to calm her a little. 'I think,' she said firmly, 'that you will make much better progress alone. Go on ahead, John George, I'll follow the crowd and see you there.'

Smith took off, dodging in and out of the crowds up Queen Street, turning left into Maiden Lane then right into Garlic Hill – where few impeded his rapid progress. Despite his bravado a nasty feeling was developing in the pit of his stomach. And it wasn't only hunger.

Chapter Eleven

The Martha huddled in a blanket before the fire in the Steam Packet public house was not the Martha Best had been talking to just before the *Bywell Castle* struck its deadly blow. This Martha was thin and fair and weeping bitterly for the baby which had been swept out of her arms as she fell into the water. Her husband and three more children she believed drowned.

Indeed, Best knew it would be a miracle for the other Martha to have survived, given where she had been sitting at the time of impact. But, nonetheless, he felt obliged to go in search of her. Partly, of course, because she had been telling him so many important things about the case, but also for decency's sake.

In a way, he felt responsible and a little guilty. If he hadn't been talking to her in that spot she might have moved and sat somewhere else. Somewhere safer. Then he deserted her just before the impact and, thereafter, had acted on the urge for self-preservation. While, deep down, his common sense told him that it wasn't his fault and he couldn't really have done anything else, he still felt guilty.

Joseph's mother wasn't in the Steam Packet pub nor was his grandpa. The landlord couldn't stop weeping. He'd been aboard the *Duke of Teck* steamboat which had trailed behind the *Princess Alice*, but had arrived in time to see some of the final, ghastly moments. His brother and sister-in-law had been aboard her. He couldn't find them and feared them lost.

W. T. Vincent was sending the first of his dispatches to London. His report, he later pointed out, was read at morning light in more than 3,000 newspapers by 'the people of every civilized land throughout the earth'.

The readers learned that, so far, only about twenty survivors had been counted and it was thought that around 500 people were lost. Afterwards, he was to claim that in this first frantic dispatch the only errors were the statement that the *Princess Alice* had been struck on the port side, when it should have said starboard – and that his estimate of the numbers lost was too conservative.

Helen arrived at the steamboat office to be greeted by a sombre Smith who averted his eyes as he informed her, 'It's pretty bad, apparently. There's been a collision with a collier. They think a lot of people have been drowned.'

'Oh, dear God.' Helen sank back against the wall. 'Dear God – why did I make him wait so long … '

Smith didn't know what to do. She had slumped down, closed her eyes and turned so pale he thought her insensible.

But, suddenly, she pulled herself up. 'Survivors. There *must* be some news … '

'There is a list,' Smith admitted carefully. 'But it's very short.'

'Yes, and … ?'

He forced himself to meet her pleading gaze and shook his head. 'He isn't on it.'

Best gazed out across the Thames. The stillness and utter silence amazed him. The smooth, moonlit Thames was only disturbed in the distance by small, dark silhouetted boats, circling the spot where the tragedy had occurred. Now and then, one of them broke away and headed back, doubtless to unload its sad cargo.

It felt almost as if the whole thing had never happened, the *Princess Alice* had never existed, never been cruelly struck, leaving people to scream and struggle for life in the water. He rubbed his tired eyes. Maybe it hadn't happened. Maybe it had all been some dreadful nightmare, a mirage, a moment in hell. If he pretended it hadn't occurred maybe it would disappear.

The idea certainly helped him to stop thinking about what he should have done or could have done, and about those he had been forced to push off the sides of the dinghy, leaving them to drown. He couldn't bear those thoughts.

'Mr Best,' called Vincent, coming up behind him. 'I've sent your telegraph to Scotland Yard. And I've just heard that about twenty-five more survivors were landed at Beckton Gasworks. There are also a few more down at Erith.'

The exhausted Best gazed at him, frowned, then for once let uncertainty show. 'I should go there and see … I don't know … if it would be better … '

'No,' said Vincent, touching Best's arm gently. 'I expect they'll send them over. Anyway, we can tap the police for names in the meantime.' Best didn't know Joseph's second name but was too tired to argue or to move.

The next couple of hours turned into a blur of unbearable sights and terrible stories: bodies brought ashore with their arms raised aloft and hands clawed, still reaching for salvation, babies and toddlers as though asleep, but asleep forever.

Male survivors told of how they had tried to save themselves and their loved ones. A young steward had leaped overboard with his ladyfriend on his back but she had slipped off as he struck out for the shore. She was not found again despite his desperate dives in search of her. A husband had jumped overboard, instructing his wife to throw their three children to him before jumping in herself, but all had been lost in the mêlée.

At three in the morning, the London Press and the first relatives arrived on the hop-pickers train, to which extra carriages had been attached. So began the swamping of this strange riverside town with anxious, bereft faces and prying eyes.

Best, back on the quayside, felt a tugging at his hand and looked down to see Joseph, now arrayed in blue-checked knickerbockers, newer than the boy's own light-brown suit but of not quite the same quality.

'He woke up and kept screaming for his mother,' George explained. 'We couldn't comfort him and we thought he might be better back with you.'

'What a splendid suit!' Best said smiling at Joseph, looking him over appreciatively. The child smiled back and held up his right foot for Best's inspection. The kind clothier obviously knew something about children for the boots were of the shiniest, black, patent leather.

Joseph was calmer once he was with Best who was surprised to find the boy had suddenly found his tongue and used it in a very confident, very precise and adult manner. The only problem was that most words were totally incomprehensible toddler talk.

The ante-room to Woolwich Steamship Company's board-room looked like a cross between a drapers and a jewellers.

Umbrellas of various sizes and colours stood to attention in the corner next to a pile of hats from derbys to fragile white straws garnished with feathers and flowers. Alongside were cane picnic boxes and baskets, and handbags. Some were neat: and simple, some fringed, some hefty and masculine, some tiny and childlike.

A clothes line festooned with shawls, capes and scarves, knitted, patterned and fringed, lent a macabre, festive look to the scene. One dramatic, black silk, shawl was emblazoned with large, yellow sunflowers while a black beaded mantle glinted as it swung gently when yet another group of grieving friends and relatives entered the room.

Small triangles of wool which had once kept children and babies warm and safe, now acted as punctuation marks between the larger shawls.

Displayed in glazed cigar boxes were watches, jewellery, cigarette cases and other small items. Each box carried a number, as did each item of clothing. The numbers corresponded with those on the bodies in the boardroom. The idea was that relatives could first try to identify the clothes and trinkets, saving them the ghastly business of searching along the lines of gruesome and foul-smelling bodies to find their loved ones. If they recognized a piece, the number would take them straight there. Once identified, the body could be put in a coffin shell for handing over to relatives.

Best had been troubled about bringing Joseph into this place but an attempt to leave him in the care of someone outside produced a flood of tears and determined little grip on his trousers.

Now, Best was desperately trying to remember what Martha and Joseph's mother had been wearing. The only sound in the quiet room was that of suppressed weeping and the clink of spurs as two army officers searched for one of their own.

'Why does everything smell so foul? They weren't in the water that long,' he said to a policeman whose depressing duty it was to act as usher. Like everyone else in the room he was holding a handkerchief to his nose in a vain attempt to block the stench.

'The outflow from those wonderful sewage palaces they blessed our manor with, and chemicals from all them Silvertown factories and gasworks,' the policeman replied grimly.

'Oh, God!' Best felt sick. 'How disgusting.' Wasn't that the final ignominy and horror – drowning in such filth?

'We've got one of our own in there.' He nodded towards the adjoining room. Obviously, he, too, was feeling the need to talk. 'Just a young fellow he is. Name of Briscoe.'

Best gazed at him, stunned. 'Not Cornelius Briscoe?'

'That's him,' the constable nodded. 'You look a bit sick. You know him?'

Best nodded dumbly. 'I'm a police officer,' he said quietly. 'I took the lad learning beats when I was on N division.' He frowned and shook his head. 'But Corny was a champion swimmer. Got a medal for saving a little boy from drowning in the Regent's Canal.'

'I 'spect he went under trying to save his wife and two kids.'

'They in there too?' Best knew Jane, a friendly and lively young woman.

He shook his head. 'No. Not been found yet.'

Best turned away in an attempt to regain control and spied an elderly blind man, feeling some trinkets from one of the cigar boxes.

'He's trying to identify his wife's jewellery,' whispered the constable.

Best's face began to crumple. He felt he could bear no more of this and stood immobile trying to pull himself together.

It was at this moment that Helen saw him. Saw her, smart, polished, alert and confident Ernest, overwhelmed. His boots were filthy, he wore a cheap, black, crumpled suit, his face was grey with shock and fatigue and a small, solemn, little boy clung to his leg.

He was alive and she had never loved him so much.

'Oh my dearest,' she said softly and held out her hands.

It was then that Best began to cry. Silently at first, then great gulping sobs rose from his chest and almost choked him as he desperately tried to hold them back.

Chapter Twelve

It was a steady beating sound and it was growing louder. Best opened his eyes cautiously. His gaze lit on a heavy oak wardrobe which he did not recognize. The mahogany chest of drawers and washstand were not familiar either. Nor the large brass oil lamp. Where was he?

His blurry eyes roamed the room: crimson wallpaper and a matching damask bed cover and heavy curtains around which only tiny slivers of light could be glimpsed. He recognized nothing. The noise was growing thunderous and was now punctuated by low voices and occasional shouts.

As he struggled out of bed he glanced down at his clothing with surprise. He was wearing a mottled grey vest and drawers. He didn't own a grey vest and drawers! He drew back the curtains. In a square below hordes of men were rushing by as if on some urgent communal errand.

'The Arsenal workers going home,' said a woman's voice. 'They've just been let out the gates.' He turned to see Helen standing by the door, his suit over her arm. His heart filled with joy at the sight of her. 'I'm told they are usually much noisier but they're trying to keep quiet – out of respect.'

'Respect?'

Then it all came rushing back. The whole terrible business. He also recalled crying and being comforted by Helen and, dimly, her bringing him here, to the Royal Mortar Hotel, and lying down beside him – along with little Joseph.

He sank down on the bed, murmuring despairingly, 'Oh God. We should have saved more! All those screaming people!' He put his hands over his ears as though to block out their cries.

She sat beside him and took his hands. 'You did what you could, dearest. I'm sure of that.'

'I had to push some of them away from the boat!'

She was silent for a moment then, holding his eye and gripping his hands, said firmly, 'You did what you had to do, you must always remember that. They tell me you saved a good many people.' She took a deep breath. 'Now we must do what we can for the living.'

He nodded and looked about him. 'Where's Joseph?'

'In the landlord's bed.'

'No one's claimed him?'

'Not yet.'

He began to reach for his clothes. 'I must find his mother.'

'You must come and have something to eat,' she said. 'Then we'll decide what to do next.'

As always, her calmness began to soothe and envelop him. Nothing was as terrible, now that she was with him. He couldn't stop looking at her. 'I'm so glad you're here,' he whispered.

She smiled, patted his hand and leaned against him. 'So am I, my love. So am I.'

'It's chaotic and dreadful out there,' said Helen. 'All those fearful and anxious relatives tramping back and forth from the Town Hall to the pier. So much sorrow. The air is thick with it.'

They were sitting in the publican's private parlour eating mutton chops and potatoes. Despite the pall hanging over him Best found he had to stop himself from gobbling it down – he felt ravenous.

He made himself pause, put down his knife and fork and reach for her hand. 'Do they know why it happened?'

She covered his hand with hers and shook her head. 'They are blaming each other. The captain of the *Bywell Castle* says the *Princess Alice* starboarded its helm when he shouldn't have done, whatever that means. The Captain of the *Princess Alice* seems to be lost so can't defend himself, but his crew says it was the *Bywell Castle*'s fault because it ported its helm. And the collier's own stoker is claiming it was because their crew was drunk.'

'They didn't seem drunk to me!'

'Maybe the accident sobered them up rather quickly.' She paused. 'Oh, and someone has told the newspapers that they didn't try to rescue anyone or throw down any ropes.'

'Now that is a lie!' exclaimed Best. 'A damned lie!' He shook his head angrily. 'Isn't it all bad enough without such nastiness!'

She nodded agreement. 'In reality, of course, no one really knows what happened yet – confusion reigns. William Vincent tells me that that part of the river has always been dangerous. There was a big collision there ten years ago. The *Wentworth* and some other ship ... '

'The *Metis*, I remember. Several people died.'

'There have been some touching tales as well,' she reassured him hurriedly. 'Down at Beckton Gasworks the freezing survivors were rushed before kiln fires by workmen who stripped them of their sodden clothes, rubbed them down, covered them over with whatever overcoats and their own clothes they could find. They took them home and later to North Woolwich, even carrying some of them on their shoulders.'

'How many have been saved?'

'They're not sure.'

'About how many?'

'A hundred,' she admitted. 'Maybe a few more. It seems a little better than they first thought.'

Best looked down at his plate and shook his head. 'There must have been six hundred, even seven ... '

Helen didn't say anything.

Best looked up, smiled wanly at her. 'We have some decisions to make.'

She took up his businesslike cue. 'Yes. I think we have.'

'I must stay and search a while longer.'

'I know, Ernest, I know.' She leaned over and stroked his cheek and touched his hair, but that brought tears to his eyes so she stopped. 'I'll take Joseph back to London and look after him until his relatives can collect him. I've given his description to the police and they'll put it in the newspapers.'

He nodded. 'I'd better telegraph Cheadle again.'

'I've done that, and sent one to Smith. He desperately wanted to come down here with me but I persuaded him he'd do more good staying in London in case you turned up there.'

'Will you go and see Cheadle as well?'

'Of course.'

'Tell him I'm still on the case so it's important that I stay.'

She raised her delicate eyebrows and put her head on one side, 'Is that strictly true, Mr Best?'

'Almost.' He grinned wickedly at her, a sight she was so pleased to see that she grinned back, even though telling fibs was not the kind of thing she would normally countenance. 'Oh, and try to stop him coming down, will you?'

'I'll do my best.' She looked rueful. 'Truth to tell he'd have difficulty finding you if you're going searching – the bodies are so spread out – they're coming up everywhere from Erith to Limehouse.'

He frowned. 'But they're all being brought back here, aren't they?'

She grimaced. 'Those from this side of the bank are, but those from the north side are not. All to do with county boundaries. The south side is in Kent and the north side is in Essex – apart from North Woolwich, that is, which, although it's on the north side, is counted as part of Kent.'

Best glanced to the heavens for help.

'Apparently it's illegal to move them from one county to another. So relatives and friends are having to find their way over muddy marshes to Beckton Gasworks, trail up Barking Creek – and so on.'

'Oh, that *is* wonderful,' said Best, 'and I thought things were already as bad as they could be.'

If Woolwich proper was a strange place, North Woolwich was even stranger, Best decided. Apart from being on the other side of the Thames and so in a different county, and yet not, it had only been in existence for about thirty years. And this showed.

Before that, the only building had been the Barge Tavern next to the ferry crossing point. The peace and solitude of the lonely marshes had been shattered when, echoing over land which had heard only the lowing of cattle and the cries of the heron, plover and bittern, came the whistle and puffing of the railway engine.

A speculator named Bidder (dubbed 'the calculating boy', due to his lightning ability to add up) had extended his Stratford and Thames Junction line down to North Woolwich in the hope that the population of Woolwich proper would cross the river by the penny ferry to ride his trains into London.

In this instance his calculations proved incorrect because, soon after, Woolwich, which had initially resisted extension of the South Eastern Railway to their town, not only welcomed it but allowed the building of not one railway station, but two.

Mr Bidder then tried to persuade people to build houses on the cheap North Woolwich land, offering them reduced rate travel as an inducement. But that didn't work either, so the railway put up money for a pleasure garden, something on the lines of Rosherville but on a much smaller scale, to be laid out along the eastern river bank.

This idea proved more successful. People did come, indeed in their thousands, but mainly during the summer months. So Bidder and his cohorts built a dock nearby, the Victoria, and were now in the process of constructing a second, the Royal Albert. Manufacturers, attracted by the cheap land and noting the twin benefits of dock and railway access, began to build factories along the riverside to the west. One of these, a Mr S.W. Silver, gave the misnomer to this bleak industrial site, Silvertown.

At last, North Woolwich began to grow. Now, several streets had been laid out, some even had houses on them. There were four pubs, a church and a tiny police station to serve the needs of its 1,500 souls, most of whom worked in the Silvertown factories or at Beckton Gasworks. But, to Best, North Woolwich still had an oddly unreal and impermanent air. It seemed a pretend, made-up place with a strange atmosphere. A place well suited to the weird and sombre scene now being enacted down by the pier.

Standing up at the front of a covered commercial wagon, alongside the carter, was a top-hatted and frock-coated gentleman. He was reading out a list of names to a large and emotional crowd who hung on his every word. Occasionally, as he spoke, someone broke into relieved sobs only to be hushed by others anxious not to miss a syllable. This was the latest news of those saved, which had been brought, post haste, from across the river.

Bidder's railway had at last achieved capacity business. Relatives and friends were pouring in from various north-London suburbs which were the catchment areas for many *Princess Alice* passengers. The idea was that, should they receive good news, via the lists of the saved, they need go no further. This arrangement was also felt to be kind and tactful in that it kept the jubilant and relieved whose loved ones had been saved, apart from the anxious who were still searching, and the devastated who had had their worst fears realized. But it wasn't entirely successful. Many relatives and friends belonged in both camps: the already bereaved and the still hopeful.

New additions to the list on this sunny September morning some thirty-eight hours after the collision were, inevitably, fewer and further between. The puzzle of how many had actually survived the collision was nearing an answer. Its solving had been drawn out due to the fact that several had been taken back to London by the *Duke of Teck*, or had made their own way, by railway. A few others had been landed at various points by small craft. Some were even swept as far downstream as the village of Erith by the *Bywell Castle*'s heavy lifeboat which, when finally launched, was able to pick up only a few and then found itself unable to make headway against the strong ebb tide. In addition, several of those saved had died shortly afterwards.

Best was waiting to hear whether Martha was called out. Smith had telegraphed her surname, Baker, to him before he left the Royal Mortar Hotel that morning. Although he was as certain as he could be that she would not be on the list, he found himself, like the rest of those gathered, clinging on to hope. It wasn't. The search for her would have to continue.

Suddenly, Best felt an iron grip on his shoulder. He was wrenched around violently. Before him – a huge, tweedy man, with a red face made puce with rage and despair.

'You let her die!' shouted Murphy. 'You callous, English bastard! You let her die!'

Best saw the blow coming too late to take more than a backward step.

Chapter Thirteen

Best was choking. He could taste blood in his mouth and someone was trying to smother him. When he managed to push the hands away a strong, sweet smell clung to his nostrils. Above him hovered a spindly old lady, anxiously bunching a large handkerchief which she was ready to reapply.

Beyond her, North Woolwich's lone constable tried to restrain a still-rabid Murphy. Warding off the smelling-salts impregnated handkerchief, Best struggled to a sitting position, spat out some blood and felt around his mouth with his fingers and tongue. His jaw was painful but, thank goodness, his teeth appeared to be intact.

'Don't worry, sir,' the young constable assured him importantly. 'This man will be charged. I saw the attack with my very own eyes.'

Several pairs of hands helped Best to his feet, then supported him once upright. He noticed that Murphy was sagging and his face was crumbling. Not from fear of him, he was sure, but from grief. Dreadful, moaning sobs emerged from his throat; sobs of a man so unused to crying that he hadn't learned how, nor been able to practise any form of restraint.

'No,' Best told the constable firmly. 'I don't want him charged.' He was careful not to shake his head as he spoke. It was thumping out its objections to any hint of movement. 'As you can see, officer, the man is grief-stricken.' He reached over, grasped Murphy's arm and squeezed it. 'He mistakenly thought I'd taken his sweetheart and then let her drown. You can't blame him.'

The PC loosened his now redundant grip. Murphy sagged. Best put his arm around him. 'I'll look after him now, Constable. He won't attack me again. Thank you for your trouble.'

His meeting with Murphy, though painful, turned out to be fruitful. The man had found and identified Martha's body. It had been back in Woolwich Dockyard, now the assembling point for all those found on the south side of the river. Best had missed it because her body had been one of a newly arrived batch washed ashore downriver at Erith.

Having had his worst fears confirmed, Murphy had been on his way back to North Woolwich railway station when he had seen Best; alive, unhurt and seemingly without a care in the world. Best, the man whom he suspected of trying to steal his sweetheart. With his good looks he had probably succeeded, then callously let her drown.

Given the circumstances, all of this was a ridiculously large assumption, but then Murphy was obviously not the brightest of men and he'd lost his love. Maybe his first, Best realized, given the man's lack of obvious charms. He'd been like a wounded lion searching for someone to maul. Anyone.

Best was not inherently dishonest but did feel that, in many respects, arbitrary truth-telling was an over-rated pastime. He quickly disabused Murphy of his suspicions, explaining that he had only ever glimpsed Martha from the garden of 9 John Street, but had certainly never spoken to her. Consequently, when he had seen her on board the *Princess Alice* (which was taking him down to see an aunt in Sheerness) he had passed the time of day with her – out of courtesy. It would have seemed rude to ignore her. But they had spoken only very briefly.

Apart from the Sheerness aunt, that was essentially true, thought Best. Anyone who might be able to say otherwise, who may even have witnessed Martha's tears, Best's comforting of her and the confessional aftermath was probably dead. If not, they almost certainly had more pressing things on their minds.

In the end, Best had made a friend out of the sad and lonely Murphy. He doubted whether the poor, simple fellow had many of those, either. It had been an easy task for someone with Best's charm to win Murphy around but he was genuinely sorry for him as well. He even considered saying that Martha had spoken of him lovingly, but pulled himself up when he realized that that might not sit well with the claimed briefness and formality of their encounter.

Maybe later he'd be able to 'recall' some chance remark that didn't seem too unlikely. Maybe the friendship would prove useful should the baby-farming investigations continue. Not that he was confident of that happening now. But, just in case, when he'd put Murphy back on his train he'd asked him to tell Mrs O'Connor to keep his room vacant until further notice.

As Best tramped along the bleak Essex shore towards Beckton Gasworks he could see the continuing activity at the collision site more closely. Out in the middle of the river a wide and ragged ring of small boats circled the spot. The flotsam, of course, had been cleared, but these boats were using a forest of long wooden poles to probe the wreck for bodies. The bright autumnal sun caused them to be thrown into silhouette against the grey-brown water, giving the scene the look of an oriental print which showed fishermen hard at work.

Bustling back and forth among the small craft the Thames Conservancy launch, *The Heron*, gathered up the latest recovered bodies before speeding off towards Woolwich Dockyard. Now and then, in the midst of all the sinister dark shapes of probing poles, boats and men, he glimpsed the rail of the *Princess Alice*'s paddle box peeping out of the water as though taunting him.

Despite the poignancy of this scene and his throbbing jaw, Best had began to feel a little more cheerful. At least part of his self-appointed task had been accomplished, even if not by him. Martha had been found. Now, only Joseph's mother and grandfather needed to be traced.

He wasn't at all sure he was being sensible in persevering with this end – the child's other relatives would probably have it in hand. Maybe they had traced them already. But he went on, nonetheless. Thinking clearly seemed to have become so much more difficult. He felt as if he'd been thrown into a whirlpool and was struggling to escape.

He still couldn't get over the suddenness of this terrible catastrophe. One minute there had been music, dancing and laughter. Children had played, then fallen asleep in their mother's arms after a wonderful day out. Then – without warning – the crushing impact. They were all in the water, thrashing about, screaming and drowning. In two or three minutes most of them had disappeared, as had the *Princess Alice*. It was just unbelievable. He had been there. He had seen it. But he still couldn't accept it had happened.

Had he *really* done all he could to help? That question kept nagging him. Yet again, he went over his actions, replaying them and changing them to what he might have done. His jaw began throbbing harder, his mouth felt sore and his eye was starting to close. He nearly lost his footing on the muddy path and crashed into the weeping man trudging along ahead of him. The cheerfulness had gone. He felt wretched.

If only he hadn't seen Martha slip out of the house the day before yesterday. Was it really only that long since he had raced down those stairs and out into the street, desperate not to lose sight of her? It seemed an eternity.

If only Cheadle hadn't stuck him there in the first place to play the invalid painter, be friendly with but not give himself away to Mrs O'Connor and her other gentlemen guests and watch poor Nella struggling to run up the garden. Dead babies, Martha, Joseph, filthy water, screams, disbelief, anguish and tears. There seemed no end to it all. Maybe he should leave now.

Best took a deep breath, placed his handkerchief over his nose and mouth and began to inspect the line of bodies on the floor of a Beckton Gasworks storage room. They were resting on boards tilted at an angle, allowing the heads and upper parts of the bodies to be viewed without having to bend over or get too close.

All the faces were blackening and bloated. All eight were female.

'They seem to be ladies of a respectable class,' murmured a chubby, overfed clergyman piously searching for members of his flock.

'Can't make much difference whether they were or not,' snapped Best with uncharacteristic sarcasm. 'Nor whether they were saints or sinners.'

The clergyman raised his eyebrows, inclined his head in a forgiving manner and murmured, 'It will in Heaven, my boy. It will in Heaven.'

Best stopped himself punching the sanctimonious cleric on the nose by dragging his attentions back to the first body, that of a stout, dark-haired lady whose ample, black alpaca-clad bosom was liberally garnished with jet. Unlike the bodies at Woolwich, most of those at Beckton Gasworks and Barking still wore their jewellery, some made more secure with safety pins to prevent loss and deter theft. Sadly, there had been some of that reported.

Next, lay a heartbreakingly tiny, fair and slight young woman of about twenty. Damp curls still clung to her forehead, her snug, black lace jacket was trimmed with black satin ribbon and, like almost all the other bodies both male and female, she wore side-spring boots. They were highly fashionable, wasn't he wearing them himself? He would imagine they were particularly difficult to kick off in the water – with that elastic gripping the ankles. Would button boots be any better? Probably not. Perhaps the only footwear easy to slip off were low shoes. He sighed.

This really was very silly and pointless, he decided – pressing on without thinking things out properly. It really was time he went back to London. He'd spent nearly all his money so didn't have much choice anyway.

There were only two bodies left and he knew that neither of them could be that of Joseph's mother. One of them wore black and the other pale brown while she, he had recalled, had been wearing a deep green ensemble. Just as he was dismissing them and turning away something familiar registered on the edge of his field of vision. He stopped and looked again.

It was a cheap tin brooch with a pale-blue enamel inset, worn at the throat of the pale brown dress. Embossed on the enamel was a crest, flags, a crown and a date: that of Queen Victoria's coronation – 1838. A common enough object – so why did it seem particularly and recently familiar? He struggled to grasp the memory. Oh yes, now it was becoming clearer. He had been shown one with pathetic pride and had felt obliged to pretend wonder.

Best frowned. But by whom? He shrugged. Who could say – it might come to him later. Certainly not by Helen nor one of his young relatives nor … He began to turn away again then froze and closed his eyes, remembering the moment. Oh *no*. It *couldn't* be. Please. It just *couldn't* be.

He forced himself to turn back and examine the body carefully. The face proved too distorted for him to identify positively but nonetheless he felt sure. Quite, quite, sure. The heavy stomach was gone but the row of safety pins down the side of the dress remained and the tear in the side of her left boot which had caused her to stumble even more as she ran back up the garden.

Nella. It was Nella. That poor child.

Oh, God. How much more of this could he take?

Chapter Fourteen

' 'Ow can you be sure it's 'er?' said Cheadle. 'You admit you couldn't tell it was 'er face.'

'I just know. The brooch, the dress, the boot … '

'All right, all right. So she went for a day on the river – just like Martha.'

'She wasn't with Martha.'

'I never said she was,' exclaimed the chief inspector irritably. 'You said she'd already left John Street so there was no reason she'd be with a girl that weren't nice to 'er, was there?' He paused. Then, as though speaking to a slow child, went on, 'So she went for a nice day out, just like everybody else did.'

'She wasn't on that boat,' Best insisted doggedly.

' 'Ow can you say that!' demanded Cheadle, then pulled back and became less aggressive. Best imagined Mrs Cheadle had instructed him to be kind to his sergeant, because he had been through such a terrible experience – but Cheadle kept forgetting. 'You was watching *Martha*, wasn't you? The boat was packed to the gunnels.' He sighed. 'Briscoe was on that boat but you never saw 'im, did you?'

He was right, of course. In theory.

Cheadle had been waiting at the Royal Mortar Hotel when Best had arrived back from Beckton that evening. Ostensibly he'd come to confer with Best about the case and check that his officer was all right. But Best knew the old warhorse couldn't resist being at the heart of things, seeing what was going on up front. He'd never lost his copper's nose nor his desire to be where things were happening – even though Mr Vincent kept telling him to spend more time supervising his men. Given all this, Best was surprised Cheadle was not being very receptive to his suspicions about Nella.

'We'll know for sure after the post-mortem,' Best said, confidently.

'A post-mortem wouldn't identify 'er,' said Cheadle stubbornly, as he cut firmly into his boiled bacon.

'No, but it should help us find out if she was murdered,' said Best, being equally stubborn.

Cheadle put down his knife and fork. 'Where's this murder idea from? These people kill babies, not the customers. That would be bad for trade – wouldn't it? We'd look a bit stupid if it got out we chased after them for killing customers!'

Ah, so that was what this was all about? Cheadle realized that Vincent looked down on him because he was ill-educated, but even Vincent had to admit the man knew about criminals. If he made a fool of himself in that direction he'd have nothing left. They might even get rid of him. Make him retire.

It wasn't only Cheadle's lack of polish that could be held against him by the grandly named Director of Criminal Investigation. There was also the fact that he had not spotted the corruption flourishing in the Detective Branch under his very nose since way back in 1873.

Of course, their original chief, Superintendent Frederick Williamson had also had the wool pulled over his eyes, but he was altogether smoother, better educated and a more acceptable chap. He had managed to come up smelling of the roses he cultivated in his spare time and to appear more sinned against than sinning. Indeed, following a Home Office enquiry he was actually promoted to chief superintendent.

What had made it even more galling to Cheadle was that previously, whenever the department was having difficulty with a case, the cry would go up that what was needed was a civilian in charge, an educated 'gentleman' civilian of course, who, due to his superior intellect, would be more able in catching murderers than stupid policemen. Indeed, a civilian in charge had been one of Vincent's recommendations to the inquiry. Well, now they'd got one – him.

Cheadle had been kept on because he was clearly honest and the newly enlarged department needed more senior officers to keep a close watch on it, not fewer.

So, it was not surprising that Cheadle was feeling less secure under their new gentleman's rule than that of the more kindly Williamson who at least had been the son of a policeman. Best tried to reassure him.

'The post-mortem will tell us how she died and we can just take it from there.'

Cheadle stared at him over the half specs Mrs Cheadle had insisted he acquire and said slowly, 'They aren't doing no post-mortems on the bodies.'

Best's head shot up. 'What do you mean? They must!'

'No they mustn't,' said Cheadle with irritating smugness. 'They done a specimen one. Found that person died of drowning – then applied it to all the others.'

Best was astounded. 'But that's ridiculous. All the murderers from miles around will be bringing their victims' bodies here and dumping them.'

'Think they'll not notice that people have been shot or had their heads battered in?' The chief inspector pushed his huge body back up from where it had slid down the chair and shrugged. 'Anyway, they 'ad no choice. There's too many bodies and they're getting more putrid by the minute.'

Best was silent for a moment, then took a deep breath. 'So, what we'll have to do is ask for a *special* post-mortem for Nella.'

'No,' said Cheadle, vehemently stabbing his last potato.
'Over my dead body.'

Best had pleaded exhaustion and escaped to his bed where he
took refuge in the newspapers. He wanted to get up to date.
He was furious at having been caught out by Cheadle over
the post-mortems. But he was also trying to distract himself
from the burning question, what to do about Nella?

In Best's experience, if one thought hard about a thorny
problem then left it, filled one's mind with other matters,
then went back to it again, with luck, solutions just popped
into one's head.

The Press was deep in the argument as to which boat was
to blame and doing much breast beating about inadequate
life-saving apparatus provided on passenger steamers.

Filling many columns were reports on where the latest
bodies had surfaced and how many, and survivors' tales.
Most of the latter, Best couldn't help noticing, related to
men. Quite a few survivors, he also noticed, were those who
at least had some idea of how to swim. Two young brothers
named Thorpe had managed to keep themselves afloat for a
long while until picked up while their sister, who had also
been taught to swim, had even struck out and reached the
river bank – an event regarded with great wonderment.
Certainly none of the women Best had seen drowning
seemed to have any idea even how to tread water, and their
heavy clothes could not have helped. He must teach Helen
how to swim as soon as possible, he told himself vehemently.

There was no child resembling Joseph's description
among those in the long and sad list of people still being
sought by relatives. But he duly made his appearance
among those found. Alongside were descriptions of two
other unidentified little boys now being cared for in the

Plumstead Infirmary. Both of these knew their names but, apparently, not where they lived, although one of them had declared that his mother sold sweets.

Best noticed that the great British letter writers had already begun sending their customary barrage of information and advice. A flag officer informed *Times'* readers that collisions on the Thames were 'incessant'. How could it be otherwise?

Steamers of all sizes and decriptions, sailing vessels, lighters, barges, and pleasure boats throng the reaches from before daylight till long after dark. Add to this fogs and mists and, not least, the smoke from factory chimneys …

Little was heard of these collisions because they occurred between smaller sailing vessels and lighters which, he claimed, never made any attempt to avoid collisions but left it to the steamers.

Given all this, no one should even contemplate going aboard a river steamer without a lifebelt. It need not be cumbrous or even unsightly – just a neat and handy cork belt fitted around the waist and over the shoulders would prove adequate to support a person in the water for hours. For females it could be made ornamental or attractive if desired.

The flag officer himself always wore an ordinary coat with an airtight lining. This could be inflated 'with his own breath' in a few seconds. He had often tried it out and it supported him and another in an upright position.

Best couldn't help but smile at the vision of the upright flag officer in his inflatable overcoat. He knew this would be the first of many such bizarre suggestions.

Thus distracted, his thoughts went back hopefully to the question of what to do about Nella, but nothing popped up nor even emerged gradually. He had been right in the first instance: the problem was insurmountable. He desperately wanted a post-mortem on Nella. Cheadle was adamant that she did not need one. Cheadle was his chief: if Cheadle said no, it was no.

Come on, said Best to himself, people are always pointing out that you have devious foreign blood in your veins; use it. Think. At last, very gradually one or two options began to suggest themselves. All of them were risky, there was no doubt. Very risky, if he wished to remain a detective at Scotland Yard and not be sent back to pound the beat among the stews of the East End. But, he felt, he had to do something for poor little Nella's sake.

Should he threaten to go to Vincent – or the newspapers? No, he couldn't do that. Should he suggest they just do a quiet inspection themselves, or possibly ask a friendly and discreet pathologist to take a look? Both these ideas could backfire, he realized. What then? He didn't know – so he thought some more and by the time he turned off the bedside oil lamp he had decided on a possible strategy.

It was a rather more relaxed and cheerful chief inspector who sat across the breakfast-table from Best this Friday morning. He was clearly enjoying his break from the Yard and doubtless felt more secure, now that the post-mortem business appeared to have been sidestepped.

Best had the sense to keep off the subject of Nella, at least for now. Instead, he described his experiences during and after the collision. The detective sergeant knew how to tell a story, and this after all, was already being described as the biggest civilian disaster in the country's history. From the moment Best recalled how, to save his life, he had had to leap on to the anchor chains, Cheadle became totally engrossed. He loved his food but when Best got to the part where he had been dragged into the water by a desperate survivor the chief inspector even allowed his bacon to cool and his egg solidify under his hovering knife and fork.

'Sounds as is you acquitted yourself well, my lad,' he said suddenly, his eyes surprisingly moist. Then, to Best's astonishment, he leaned over and patted him on the arm.

Given the sequence of events, it seemed quite natural that they should arrive at the subject of bodies. The forward part of the *Princess Alice* had been raised on Wednesday, the day after the collision. Many bodies had come with it – all of people who had been trapped in the saloon deck. These included a soldier in the 11th Hussars; the barmaid, who had £3 takings in her pocket, and a young woman with a little boy clinging around her neck, his toy trumpet entangled in her hair.

As these bodies were being brought out and transferred to *The Heron*, Best related, there had been a sinister and dramatic moment. The *Bywell Castle* had steamed by on its way to the sea – on board, a new captain and crew.

More to the point was that today, Friday, they were to attempt to tow the fore part to the south bank when further bodies would probably be discovered. The authorities were also planning to try to raise the larger and heavier aft part wherein even more sad discoveries would be made.

'It'll be mayhem here again today,' Best said. 'And the weekend will bring more droves of sightseers,' he took a deep breath. 'So, I suppose we'd better hurry and get a message sent to Islington police asking them to call at John Street to find out how we can contact Nella's family.'

Cheadle's toast halted abruptly *en route* to his mouth. His eyes narrowed. 'You said,' he enunciated slowly, 'that you couldn't say definitely it was her.'

'No. That's right,' Best admitted innocently, 'that's why we need her family to identify her, isn't it?'

'But if you can't identify her and she ain't in the lists of the missing ... '

'There are plenty of other unidentified bodies which nobody seems to be claiming. It's obvious that some people don't even realize that their relatives went on the trip. If we can, we should let them know.'

'But if you can't say—'

'I recognized the brooch.'

'Ten a penny.' Cheadle's face was reddening.

'And the dress.'

'Common as muck.'

'Her hair colour is similar as well, and the way she wears it.'

'Mousy and scraped back, I bet. Don't mean nothing.'

Best sighed. 'And, of course, I'll have to mention finding her in my report – seeing as how Nella comes into it earlier.'

'All right! All right!' Cheadle exploded. 'As long as you're dropping this stupid murder business!'

'I'd like to,' said Best with pained sincerity. 'I really would. But when Mr Williamson and Mr Vincent read what she said when I last spoke to her, they're bound to wonder why I … '

The chief inspector looked as if he was about to have a heart attack. His eyes bulged and choking sounds came from his mouth. Eventually he forced the words out very, very slowly, 'What – she – said?'

'Yes,' said Best guilelessly, shaking his head as though he wished he wasn't always so obliged to tell the truth.

'Tell me,' said Cheadle through gritted teeth, '*what* – the – woman – said.'

Best took a deep breath. 'She said, "I'm afraid of them. If they sees me talking to you they'll kill me".' He shook his head again, sadly. 'I thought maybe it was just her imagination – her being so young and all … or it could be just a figure of speech. But there was real fear in her eyes, terror even and—'

'All right! All right!' snapped Cheadle. 'Don't over-egg the pudding! This ain't the Alhambra on a Saturday night!'

'You're such a terrible fibber, young Best,' exclaimed a laughing Helen. 'It will get you into no end of trouble one day!'

Then she grew serious. 'Do you really think that poor girl was' – she mouthed the word 'murdered' just in case Joseph woke up. He was asleep in Best's arms, having refused to leave his side since he arrived at Helen's house that evening. Joseph wouldn't know what it meant but might make it one of his favourite new words, some of which came out clearly even if those around it made no sense.

'I don't know, really I don't. But it seemed so odd her being there at the gasworks. I could swear she wasn't on the boat,' he shrugged, 'but I could be wrong – there were so many on the way back.'

They both sat silent for a minute. The horror of it once again sweeping back unbidden, accompanied by disbelief. The number drowned was now thought to be about 650. But nobody really knew and probably never would, it was admitted.

Best nodded down to Joseph. 'Still no claimants?'

She shook her head. 'Not one.' She pushed a strand of hair out of her eyes and looked at him. 'I'm not sure what we are going to do if no one comes for him.'

'How has he been?' Best asked, when the sleeping Joseph had finally been spirited away and the kissing had stopped for a moment.

'Cries for his mother a lot, of course. But sometimes, if we can distract him with toys and games, he will play happily for a while.'

They were sitting side by side in her parlour. She turned to look at him. 'I notice that some of the children's homes have offered to take the orphans.'

Best looked at her, aghast. 'We couldn't do that to Joseph. We're all he's got!'

'I didn't say we should! But we need to think about all the possibilities. We're in no position to keep him, are we – and Dr Barnardo's has a very good name … ' Her face had grown pink and her eyes angry.

Best said nothing. This took them back to the very reason they were not yet married. Why she had made him wait so long. Did this mean she was not going to marry him after all? He just couldn't bear to ask just then. How could he have become so fond of such a hard-hearted woman!

She read his thoughts and turned on him. 'I want to paint!' she exclaimed angrily. 'Just like you want to be a detective! Why is that so hard to understand?'

Chapter Fifteen

The nineteen inquest jurors were culled largely from Powis Street, Woolwich's most important business venue and its surrounds. They included two silversmiths, an upholsterer, a milliner, an auctioneer, a grocer, a bootmaker, a carriage dealer and a publican.

It was six days after the collision and all were ranged around the long oval table in the meeting-room of the Town Hall. Occupying the centre chair was Mr Charles Joseph Carttar who had served as West Kent coroner for no less than forty-six years, having succeeded his father in the post at the age of twenty-one. Carttar's mind was still sharp. Indeed, he had presided over the celebrated inquest on Harriet Staunton at Penge only the previous year, as a result of which four persons had later been convicted of starving the poor girl to death.

However, Carttar had become a little pedantic over his long years in office and he was no longer a well man. Heart trouble sometimes caused him to become breathless and he was now less agile than the job sometimes demanded. This particular inquest was certainly not helping matters. Like his jurors, he already looked exhausted and there was still a very long way to go. Nonetheless, they all managed to look with kindness and sympathy at the man standing before them.

Wilhelm Berger's jet-black hair clung to his head as though wet. He was, Best noticed, a chunky, square-shaped man in most respects. His square block of a head sat low on his square, solid body, and his hands, with their short stubby fingers, made up another, smaller, square. In them, he continuously twisted a check cap which had seen better days. Wilhelm was obviously much poorer than many of the other victims' relatives. His dark suit was of a cheap fustian. At his throat, a knotted black and white check neckerchief and on his feet he wore heavy, studded, Blucher boots which, to his obvious embarrassment, had resounded noisily on the parquet floor as he approached.

The police sergeant hovering behind Wilhelm was, by now, well versed in the unique procedure of this inquest.

'I never knew she vos gone down the river, Your Vorship,' explained Wilhelm. 'I'm not knowing vere she got the money, I'm sure.' He paused and glanced at the policeman to see whether he was saying the right things. The policeman gave an almost imperceptible nod and Wilhelm carried on. 'That's vy I never come forward sooner you see. I didn't know.'

'I assure you, Mr Berger,' said Mr Carttar leaning forward, 'you are not alone in that. Others have found themselves in a similar predicament and, indeed, judging by the number of poor souls still unidentified, many remain so.'

Wilhelm Berger nodded glumly, unsure of whether he was expected to respond.

'As long as you are sure she is your daughter, Miss Helen Berger, that is the most important thing at the moment.'

Wilhelm dragged a dingy handkerchief from his pocket and dabbed at his eyes before murmuring brokenly, 'I am, Your Vorship, I am. God bless my poor little Nella!'

'You have our deepest sympathies,' Mr Carttar gently assured him.

Best knew that Wilhelm Berger had at first not been quite so sure, probably and understandably reluctant to admit his loss, but had obviously now realized that the girl was indeed his Nella.

The coroner leaned forward and addressed him again. 'As you may know, Mr Berger, our principal task at this stage is to hear evidence of identification so that the bodies may be released to relatives who may then have them buried here at Woolwich or take them for burial nearer home. I will issue a certificate to you so you may claim the body. The bulk of the victims will be registered as drowned, as they so clearly were, but we will be taking more evidence with regard to one or two of the deceased, to satisfy legal needs as regards to all of them, until after we have concluded the next part of our inquest on the cause of the accident. Nella will be one of those.'

Wilhelm Berger was confused and again looked towards the police sergeant for help.

'Don't be concerned, Mr Berger,' said the coroner. 'You may take Nella's body and have it interred. This is merely a legal formality.'

'Oh, yes, I understand.' His face cleared. 'Thank you sir.' He looked about him now unclear as to whether to commence his thunderous exit. The policeman placed a guiding hand on his arm and led him away.

Outside, Best caught up with him. Bodies from both sides of the river were now being held in the dockyard. The drill, Best had ascertained, was that the relative took his certificate there, whereupon the body would be moved from the unidentified to the identified shed, placed in a simple, light coffin and handed over.

It was universally acknowledged that these arrangements had worked remarkably well, considering how mammoth was the task. They had been organized by the police authorities whose representatives had now been issued with smelling salts in a vain attempt to keep the stench from their nostrils. This onerous heavy work was carried out by both dock labourers and soldiers from the nearby barracks.

However, it had now been decreed that the unidentified bodies were in such a state of putrefaction that they could be held no longer and, if necessary, they were to be buried unrecognized. From now on, carefully labelled belongings and photographs of the dead were to be the only means of recognizing a loved one. The removal had already begun which meant Best and Wilhelm had to move with some speed to be in time to prevent Nella going nameless to her grave.

As Best and Wilhelm arrived at the dockyard, several ambulance wagons, driven by soldiers in full dress uniform, were already proceeding slowly along the alley leading from the gates. The day's first consignment of unidentified bodies was on its way to be buried. A snaking line of private corteges followed.

Best helped to speed Wilhelm Berger through the procedure, making sure that although Nella's coffin was loaded on to an army wagon it was clearly marked with her name. Then he found them a cab which tagged on to the rear of the sombre procession.

They trundled slowly past hushed, respectful crowds lining Woolwich's shuttered streets. Nella's father sobbed quietly all the while. At the Arsenal Gates they turned right on to the Plumstead Road, then soon began the climb towards Woolwich New Cemetery which was set on a hillside nearly two miles from the town.

In an onrush of pity, *The Times* had described this graveyard as 'a pretty place, shaded by many trees, bright with flowers planted among the graves, and fragrant with the odour from its cedars, limes, and Italian pines'.

Perhaps it could be all of those things, but to Best that day it was like a scene from hell. Mounds of black earth loomed over a hundred new graves and the ground between them was dark with coffins, gravediggers, clergymen, sightseers and unconsolable mourners.

Endless sobs and agonized wailing filled the air – punctuated every now and then by the mournful sound of a ship's siren drifting up from the river below. On the crest of the hill, like an omniscient presence, stood a surpliced

clergyman starkly outlined against the backdrop of a dark
and lowering sky.

'Be ye also ready,' he was almost bellowing at the groups
of people scattered around the graves of the unclaimed,
'for no man knoweth the hour, and souls redeemed by
the Saviour's love could cheerfully face even sudden death
were they always ready for the Master's call!'

Best doubted that.

He noticed that some of the labourers were having trouble
fitting the coffins into the graves, despite the fact that both
coffins and the holes in the ground had been widened to
cope with the swollen state of the bodies. A final ignominy.

By now, Wilhelm Berger's stubbly black beard was
sodden with his tears and he could only stumble blindly as
Best led him alongside Nella's coffin to a spot near one of
the pines. A lady was throwing handfuls of sweet-smelling
flowers on to the coffins of the nameless. Best asked for
some to scatter on to Nella's plain box as it was lowered
into the cold ground.

'I will avenge you, poor child,' he murmured as he did
so. 'I will. I promise.'

Somehow, his dramatic uttering did not seem in the least
strange in such an awful place.

Best suddenly felt he needed to know more about the
life of the young girl they had just laid to rest, but he was
endeavouring to contain his curiosity. To rush in would
not only be unseemly, it would be unfeeling – Berger
might unravel altogether.

He waited until Nella's father had taken a few reviving
gulps of London porter before murmuring quietly, 'Whew,
that was an ordeal.'

'*Ja. Ja.*' Berger nodded and wiped his mouth with the
back of his hand. 'It vos not very nice up there.' He paused.
'I not be able to do it without you.'

'It was the least I could do. I liked her.'

Berger looked puzzled. 'You know my Nella well?'

'Oh no.' Best shook his head. 'I just happened to be staying next door in John Street.'

Wilhelm hung his head. 'Dat vos shaming.'

'No.' He patted the man's hand. 'She was a nice girl. These things happen.'

'So you are knowing Mrs Dawes then?'

'Oh, no. I just saw Nella once or twice when I was out in the garden next door. I was painting my watercolours and she was hanging out clothes. We just passed the time of day.'

Berger knitted his brows. 'You paint pictures? That's a job?'

'No,' Best smiled. 'I've been ill, you see, and I was recuperating. I just do it to pass the time.'

'I don't know vot ve will do vithout Nella.'

'I expect your wife is very upset.'

'Mv vife is dead.'

'Oh, I'm sorry.'

'No.' He spread his chunky, calloused hands. 'How you know that?' He sighed. 'Nella, she looked after me and the children.'

'Have you many other children?'

'Four. They are very sad.'

Best knew Berger was a building labourer and wondered how he could have afforded Mrs Dawes's fees.

'It must have been hard on you – her staying with Mrs Dawes and then having to pay the fees as well.'

Berger nodded. 'She charge a lot.' Then he grinned, startling Best. 'But I got special price.'

'Oh?'

He shrugged, causing his head to sink even lower into his chest. 'I know Mrs Dawes from a long time.'

'Oh, well. That must have been a help.'

'It vos. It vos.'

'And the father chipped in, I hope?'

'Father? Vot father?'

'Of Nella's baby?'

A cautious look entered the man's eyes. 'I not know who he is.'

'She never told you?'

'No.'

'You had no idea?'

He shook his head and shrugged again. 'Who knows? Could be anyone. Zat boy she liked down the road – they got behind a shed maybe. The milkman in our kitchen while I not there. I dunno!' He seemed suddenly agitated so Best shrugged as well and retreated behind his glass of ale.

He knew little about Wilhelm Berger apart from the fact that he lived near the Caledonian Road, which wasn't very far from John Street. This made it just a little odd that he had moved Nella there. Most people wanted to hide a shameful pregnancy so booked into somewhere some distance from their homes. Maybe it was the special price which had been the decider.

One thing he did know about Nella's father: he had fallen foul of the law at some stage. Addressing the coroner as 'Your Vorship', was a sure sign. But then many immigrants got themselves into little scrapes, often fairly minor, through ignorance or their dire straits.

'I not understand this man who say Nella will be held back. That she not drown.'

'No, no. He didn't say that,' Best insisted. He suddenly felt very very tired but took a deep breath and launched forth. 'Look, it's difficult to explain but – just so they don't have to examine all the bodies thoroughly to find out what killed them – which they really know was drowning after the accident. They are examining only one or two and using them as specimen cases, just in case the rest of the investigation reveals anything further – such as it being a deliberate collision or caused by negligence – which could mean a charge of manslaughter.' Best stopped to gather his resources. 'He is holding on to one or two cases so he can add things to their certificates if necessary,' he finished.

Best wasn't surprised the man looked even more confused as a result of his garbled explanation. He was, himself.

'But vy my Nella?' he asked eventually. 'Vy her?'

'I don't know,' Best lied. 'It could be that he has selected one young girl and one young boy, then a middle-aged woman and a middle-aged man. I've heard it's something like that,' he lied again. 'Others have been held back – the ones whose relatives are suing the company and have lawyers at the inquest. They have been held back.'

That was true. It was also true that the coroner was basing his specimen enquiries around only one victim, William Beechey, the first person whose body had been identified.

'It is very peculiar, this "specimen",' said Berger.

'I know. I know.'

Best hesitated, wondering whether he should tell Berger about their suspicions. Hadn't he the right to know? But wouldn't that complicate matters terribly as well as alerting suspects?

'It is because I'm foreign.'

'No! Good heavens, no!'

He was not convinced. 'I dunno … '

'Look, I don't understand it all completely, but this is a very unusual inquest and inquiry as it has been a very unusual accident and they're making up procedure as they go along.' Best patted his hand. 'You've got your Nella buried, that's the main thing. Go home and look after your other children. I'll see if I can get you some help from the Lord Mayor's Fund.'

It was true, Best didn't really understand all the ramifications but he did know that Carttar the coroner had done his bit by including Nella on his case-to-be-kept-open list and seen to it she had a post-mortem. It was up to them now.

Chapter Sixteen

'You've got to go back in,' Cheadle announced in his usual blunt fashion. 'There's been more bodies and we've 'ad another letter saying that that lot in John Street are still at it.' He held up the familiar, blue speckled writing-paper.

It didn't surprise Best to know they were 'still at it'. Martha had told him as much. She'd told him that, at first, she'd believed Mrs Dawes when she'd said that soon after birth the babies were taken to a house in Finsbury where they were put up for adoption. After a while, however, she had begun to find it curious that they disappeared from the scene so quickly, even if born in the middle of the night.

When questioned, Mrs Dawes had laughed and said that that just showed how efficient they were. But minor incidents began pointing to a different story and Martha started to take notice of the other servants' dark hints. Then, quite by accident, she'd been there at a birth and had caught Mrs Dawes and Dr Helman actually smothering a new-born. Mrs Dawes's brazen response had been to declare that now Martha was party to the whole business and just as likely to hang as them.

The poor girl had felt trapped. She needed the job to support her son. Soon after, they had asked her to 'drop' little bodies. They offered her extra money for the task, money she could save to educate little Georgie, to give him a chance in life.

Why can't we keep the babies and advertise them for adoption, she'd pleaded? But Mrs Dawes claimed that they had tried that for a while, but it had proved too difficult. Supply exceeded demand, so they were constantly left with spare babies on their hands, babies for which they had neither the room nor the staff to cope. Besides, the little creatures were noisy and inclined to smell, which was bad for the business.

Not only that, further care cost money. As did the advertising and clothing to make them look halfway decent and appealing to prospective adoptees. This ate into the lump sums they received from the clients for taking the problem off their hands. Often, quite substantial sums were handed over, Martha revealed, so that the women could walk away relieved of their burdens and pretend nothing had happened.

In any case, Mrs Dawes had insisted, so many babies died at birth – or soon after – what did a few more matter? Indeed, how few children actually reached adulthood? Think of the heartache they saved. Looking at it like that, they could almost be said to be doing a public service.

Despite the fact that Best had half-known what was going on, he'd been horrified – and even more determined to stop the killings. But so many terrible things had happened since he had spoken to the tearful Martha and he was sick of the whole business. So much baby-farming went on anyway with a greater or smaller degree of evil intent that this case was merely a pinprick and it seemed to him now that solving it would achieve little.

Most of all, he was sick of living at John Street and of playing the artistic invalid. He wanted to get back to his own life with his colleagues – and to Helen. This all raced through his mind as he faced his chief inspector, took a deep breath, and asked, 'Can't we try another approach, sir? That one didn't work very well last time and—'

'No,' snapped Cheadle. 'We can't "try another approach",' he mimicked. 'It would waste all that work. Anyway, you're in a better position now. You've got an in, next door.'

Best cleared his throat. 'Maybe new blood might be more successful. Littlechild maybe. I could say he was my cousin.'

'Littlechild's 'elping Greenham with the Russian rouble forgeries.'

Oh, very important. The Russian Government had been complaining about rouble forgery for years. The Yard knew they were churned out by Poles and Russians in the East End but they'd never had much luck nailing them – they were too clever and their gangs frightened people. They'd only ever caught smaller fry.

'They've caught some of the big boys,' grinned Cheadle triumphantly, 'an' are on the tail of a lot more. The Russian Government is very pleased.'

Ah, that was it. Large rewards were to be had.

The discussion had begun with the usual quibbles about expenses which had landed him out of pocket once again despite the claims of improvement since the Commission's recommendations last year. He felt even more worn out.

I've had enough of this, Best thought. There must be some another way to earn a living. Overlooked in the new promotions. Why bother? Hand in my notice. Why not?

But what about the pledge over Nella's grave? He could investigate that in his own time, he decided. That was it.

'Sir,' he began firmly and there wasn't a good deal of respect in his eyes. 'Sir ... I—'

'Get them in John Street sorted out,' Cheadle said, 'an' we'll have this Nella business settled, too.'

Best said nothing which was almost tantamount to insubordination.

'You can 'ave two or three days off first,' Cheadle conceded, obviously sensing rebellion. 'Not too long, mind you, or the trail will go cold.'

Best took a deep breath. It was no good. He'd made up his mind. 'Look, sir,' he said, 'It's no use—'

Cheadle interrupted again. 'You wouldn't want to leave a job 'alf finished, would you, *Inspector* Best?'

The old bugger!

'Just come through while you was in Woolwich.' He pushed his huge body upright once again, picked up a copy of Police orders and waved it at Best. 'Congratulations, son!' He put out his hand. The old war horse was grinning all over his face, secure once again in his own guile and the ability to outsmart others.

Helen was in her studio when Best arrived. He loved it in there and was so proud of her talent and fascinated by her work. She was just finishing up, cleaning her brushes and hands – so was at his mercy.

'Sergeant Best!' she exclaimed, as he got her in his grasp.

'Inspector, if you don't mind,' he murmured casually into her hair. 'Let's have a little respect, woman.'

Her face lit up in a wide smile. 'Oh, that's wonderful,' she exclaimed. 'About time they showed their appreciation.'

He refrained from revealing the bad news, the return to John Street, just yet. No sense in spoiling the moment and she was obviously delighted for him and, he was pleased to see, seemed quite proud of him.

'What do you think,' she said, when they stopped the kissing so she could finish cleaning up. She pointed to her easel.

'Good heavens,' he said. 'It's Joseph!'

She laughed. 'I'm glad you recognize him. It's just an underpainting as yet, of course. A long way to go.'

'You'll be stuck if he is claimed before it's finished?'

'That's not very likely I fear.'

Despite continuing police enquiries, it transpired that none of Joseph's other relatives had yet surfaced.

'He must surely have some aunts and uncles,' said Helen. 'I think I've picked out an Auntie May from among his burbles. I've told the police and they've put it in the newspaper again – so we could be hearing soon.'

'If we don't, perhaps we should keep him,' said Best hopefully. He was becoming fond of the precise little boy who held his head so straight, except when the subject of his mother came up. Then it slumped on to his chest and the tears ran down and soaked his shirt and sobs racked his pathetically small frame. Besides, he and the little lad had been through a lot together. There was also the possibility that keeping Joseph might hurry along the prospect of marriage.

Joseph had obviously become fond of Helen. Fascinated even. He followed her around just staring at her. A bit like me, Best thought ruefully. She was kind and thoughtful with the boy, reading to him and letting him splash around with watercolours. But it was her housekeeper who supplied most of the necessary supply of hugs and sang to him when she put him to bed. Had Helen no mothering instinct, Best wondered? Or was she holding it back?

One thing was certain: she was not happy that he had to go back to John Street. 'Just when we were getting a chance to renew our acquaintance,' she said crossly. He didn't much like the sound of that "acquaintance". 'And to see how we feel, and make our decisions,' she added.

He knew how he felt and what his decision was and said so. Could it be that she didn't love him? No. He knew that couldn't be true. Since he had come back their passion for each other had almost gained full sway. They hated to be apart and, when together, gazed at each other and touched constantly.

'We must discuss things,' she said, when he brought up marriage. 'As soon as Joseph has been claimed and you are back from Islington.' She paused thoughtfully. 'Is there nothing you can do to hurry all that business along?'

He shook his head. 'We must have solid evidence and daren't rush things in case they take fright and decamp. It's happened before and a lot of time and money have been wasted.'

It did shock him that she seemed not to be as horrified as he by the baby-farming and consequent 'child dropping'.

'What do you expect?' she had said crossly, when they were discussing it. 'What choice do some of these poor women have!' But she did think that the murder of Nella was a terrible thing and, in fact, became quite emotional about it. 'We must do something,' she agreed.

'Oh, but it's been just terrible around here,' exclaimed Mrs O'Connor, as she ladled out the Irish stew. 'So many of them came from Islington. The place has been a vale of tears!' Best had read about the young lady from Barnsbury Street, the landlord of the Alfred Tavern, where Best had supped an occasional pint with Smith, and the landlord's two sons – all gone.

'Most of that Cowcross Street Bible Class came from round here,' she said. 'Over forty of them there were, and only three came back.'

'I think it must have been them I heard singing hymns just before the collision,' said Best.

She sighed and shook her head. 'The really sad bit,' she said, handing him his plate, 'is that the outing was all so last minute. That Miss Law had been promising them all the treat, them being so poor and her so wealthy, and when she saw what a lovely day it was she sent round a message saying "Today's the day".' She paused in her ladling. 'It certainly was, wasn't it? For her too, and her friends she'd asked along.'

'Makes you wonder,' said Best.

'What God above is thinking of?' she nodded. 'You're right. And as for that poor child Nella!'

Best nodded. 'I had expected to find Martha's body because I'd seen her on board – but when I found Nella's as well, I just couldn't believe it!'

'Such a shock it must have been. The poor lamb.' She sat down at the table. 'I can imagine.' She shook her head, 'No, no, in fact, I can't. Truly, it beggars belief.'

Best looked up quickly and frowned before dragging his attention back to his meal.

'That Murphy's been beside himself over Martha. I didn't even know he knew the girl. Never met her myself.' She sighed. 'One can't help thinking there's a bit of the judgement of the Lord in there – but I suppose that's too uncharitable.'

Best pretended he didn't know what she was talking about. One thing was sure, he was relieved that Murphy wasn't in the house. He'd gone to Ireland to see his family and was not due back for a couple of days.

Mrs O'Connor gave him a penetrating look. 'Sure, and weren't we worried about you as well – particularly you being an invalid and all.' She handed him the salt. 'I must say I was surprised at you dashing off down the river in the first place. Then, when you didn't come back and we heard about the terrible tragedy, we thought without doubt you must have perished along with all the others.'

Best tried to look casual. 'Well, it was such a nice day, I acted on the spur of the moment. I lived to regret it.' He realized how that sounded and added. 'But, at least I lived.'

'You were lucky, very lucky.' She gave him a long look. 'I think perhaps you must be stronger than you think, wouldn't you say?'

'If I am, Mrs O'Connor,' he said, 'it's probably down to your good feeding.'

She smiled back at him, but there was doubt in her eyes. He was, he realized, up against someone hard to fool and to charm. He'd been right: Littlechild should have come here instead of himself.

Young Linwood, who had been straining forward in his seat just dying to ask questions, could bear it no longer.

'What was it like when you saw the collier looming up on you like that?'

'Bloody terrifying. Excuse the language, Mrs O'Connor, but I've never been so frightened in my life.'

'So, what did you do!'

'I jumped on to its anchor chains.' The moment he said it he realized it was a mistake.

'And you being so weak,' mumured Mrs O'Connor. 'Who'd have thought it possible?'

'They say fear gives you the strength of ten, Mrs O'Connor,' he explained.

'It seems so.'

Young Linwood was agog. 'Is it true that hardly anyone could swim? That they all drowned in seconds?'

Best looked down at his stew and closed his eyes in a vain attempt to lock out the flailing bodies pushing each other under and screaming such terrible screams.

'If you go on like this, Mr Linwood,' scolded Mrs O'Connor, 'I'll be thinking that my food is not good enough to occupy your attention.'

Linwood couldn't contain his curiosity, 'No, but, they say they all struggled and—'

'Mr Linwood!' she exclaimed sharply. 'Have some sense! Can't you see the man's upset!'

Best realized he'd been grasping his spoon with awful ferocity but that hadn't stopped it rattling against his plate, a reaction which startled even him. He was glad when supper was over and took the opportunity to excuse himself so he could go up to his room to write a letter to his cousin.

When he got there, he stopped outside the door for a moment, kept quite still and listened. Detecting no sound behind him he carried on up the next flight of stairs, halted before his landlady's room, turned the handle of her door and slipped inside. She should be in her kitchen yet awhile, clearing up the supper things.

Mrs O'Connor's room was quite small and modest. Apart from the single bed with its rose-strewn cover there was space only for a simple, rather shabby oak wardrobe and a small chest of drawers. Would he find what he was looking for here, or had she somewhere else for her odds and ends, Best wondered?

The left-hand top drawer yielded only plain handkerchiefs and black lisle stockings. The second appeared a little more promising. Heaped higgledy-piggledy were small boxes of mementoes; a tiny faded silk rose, a jet necklace he'd seen his landlady wearing on Sunday evenings and a blue enamelled brooch bearing a portrait of a young Queen Victoria.

He glanced behind him, straining to catch any hint of sound on the stairs, then lifted out all the small items so he could reach and remove the flat, red, writing folder beneath. With shaking hands he opened it – and there it was.

'Would it just be my jewellery you're after, Mr Best,' said a cold voice behind him. He froze. 'If it is, you'll see there's not much of it.'

He turned round slowly, his face scarlet, cursing himself that, in his excitement, he'd failed to keep proper watch. What to do now?

As they stared at each other he took a deep breath before holding up the blue speckled writing-paper. 'No, Mrs O'Connor,' he said quietly, 'it was this.'

She put her head to one side. 'If you'd run out of paper you had only to ask,' she said. 'No need—'

He cut her short. 'It was you, wasn't it?'

'If you're wanting to know if I wrote those letters to Scotland Yard.' She shrugged and smiled wryly. 'Yes, *Officer*, it was me.'

Chapter Seventeen

They stayed up late, talking. Best explained that while an expression she used, 'it beggars belief', had chimed with him, he had been unable to pinpoint why. Indeed, the penny hadn't even dropped when he'd read the second letter, where she had used it again. It was only that evening, when she'd said it at supper, that it all fell into place.

'Sure,' she sighed, 'I haven't the makings of a spy, have I now?'

Best smiled and shook his head. 'You've been a great help to us pinpointing this place. Now, all we need is enough evidence.'

'I'll help you all I can.'

That was what he wanted to hear. It was the hope she would say that which had made him take the chance of bearding her.

'I have to say, you never looked very poorly to me,' she confessed with a grin. 'And when I spotted you dashing off after Martha like that, I thought to myself – Mrs O'Connor, if only you were that sick!'

She agreed to keep watch when Best was out and to make a note of what she saw. Also, to give evidence if necessary. He couldn't ask for more than that. But he did.

'We're going to have to make friends with them.'

She looked aghast. 'I don't know if I could do that.'

'I'm sure you could, Mrs O'Connor. I don't mean become bosom pals – just casually pass the time of day. Then build on that. I'll be starting in the morning when I go to see them.'

'You're going in there?' said his new recruit doubtfully. 'Won't that be giving the game away?'

'No. It would be more suspicious if I didn't. They must know I was the last to see Martha alive. I'll just be offering my condolences and saying how happy she looked – just before ... '

'And Nella? What will you say about her?'

'I don't know yet. I'll think about that.'

Next morning Best presented himself at the door of 7 John Street. It was a fresh, sunny but very still day with just a hint of early autumn musty sharpness in the air.

A thin, young skivvy of about fourteen opened the door.

'I'm from next door,' he told her. 'I'd like to see your mistress, please.'

The lank-haired girl looked doubtful but had obviously received some instruction in how to handle unexpected callers. She led him to the front parlour before taking his name and saying she'd see whether Mrs Dawes was in.

'She doesn't know me,' he warned, 'but tell her it's about Martha. I was on the *Princess Alice*.'

The girl's pale-blue eyes widened and her already slack mouth dropped further open. She tried to mumble something but was too confused to get anything out.

It was some minutes before a well-upholstered, middle-aged woman appeared, wearing an expression of pious sadness on her plump face but with a wariness in her faded blue eyes. She must have been a peaches and cream beauty once, thought Best, and there was still something about her.

'Mr Best,' she said, holding out her hand. 'I'm Mrs Dawes. Mary says you knew our poor, dear Martha.' Her voice was straining for gentility.

'Well, not exactly,' he said, shaking her hand. 'I'd only seen her occasionally coming and going from here. I'd never actually spoken to her but, of course, when we recognized each other on the *Princess Alice* we exchanged a few words. Out of politeness really. As one does.'

'Of course, of course.'

She sat him down on the sofa, placed herself alongside on a matching armchair and pulled out a lacy handkerchief. A waft of eau de Cologne assailed his nostrils. 'That poor girl,' she exclaimed, 'I still can't believe it. She was like a daughter to me.'

He nodded sympathetically. 'It was a terrible thing. Terrible. I have nightmares.'

'Oh, you must. You must.' She paused before asking tremulously, 'Were you with her when ... please tell me all about it. I must know the worst.'

That was what most people wanted to hear, Best had found. However, he had already decided that in this instance the full drama and the (almost) truth, would most suit his purposes.

'The awful thing is that it was just before the collision happened when we spoke. We'd only just said hello and something about recognizing each other from John Street, when there was all this commotion at the front of the boat. I went forward to see what it was all about, leaving poor Martha sitting there, all unsuspecting just by the paddle box. Suddenly, to my astonishment and horror I saw the *Bywell Castle* – its great red hull looming above us. Then it just crashed into us – by the paddle box – near where Martha had been sitting!'

'Oh!' Mrs Dawes exclaimed thrusting the handkerchief up to her putty nose and loose mouth. 'Oh, my goodness!'

Best looked alarmed and reached forward to clasp her hand. 'Oh, my dear lady! How tactless of me to tell you that. I should never ... '

'No,' she reassured him, rapidly recovering herself as she patted her chest to still her heart. 'I must hear the truth, hard though it may be. I owe it to the poor girl's memory.'

Best shook his head and made a show of not knowing how to continue.

'And then ... ' Mrs Dawes prompted him.

He inclined his head sadly. 'The bow chains of the *Bywell Castle* were hanging there before me and, without thinking, I just leaped on to them and was pulled to safety.'

'Oh, oh,' she said.

'I didn't think. I didn't think,' he exclaimed in distress, 'about Martha – about leaving her like that!'

'But I'm sure you couldn't have done anything, my boy,' Mrs Dawes reassured him, her pale chins wobbling in sympathy.

'I know. I know,' he agreed. His voice broke a little as he spoke. 'But I still feel guilty, so guilty.'

'Oh, you mustn't, you mustn't,' she said, a trifle impatiently. For a second, her pious expression slipped as she leaned forward eagerly. 'Was it as bad as they say?'

'Oh, dreadful. Quite dreadful.'

He had just begun to elaborate further when the doorbell rang, followed shortly afterwards by a knock on the parlour door and a girl's voice saying, 'The doctor's 'ere', Mrs Dawes.'

Her mistress was clearly very torn by this news, as was Best who was only just warming up.

'Tell him to go through, Lizzie,' Mrs Dawes replied, 'I'll be with him in a moment.' She turned to Best. 'I must know more about poor Martha's fate,' she said, 'I owe her that.' She dabbed her eyes. 'Can you come back tomorrow at tea-time – about four o'clock?'

Best nodded. 'Of course, dear lady. Of course.' This was just what he wanted. A further visit would consolidate their acquaintanceship, then all he would need was some other reason to drop in again – in neighbourly fashion.

'She obviously likes to give the premises a respectable air,' he told an eager Mrs O'Connor when he got back. 'The front parlour is quite genteel and she's trained the girl Lizzie a little on how to receive callers.'

'Did you see that doctor fella close up?' asked Mrs O'Connor conspiratorially.

'Only a glimpse. No more.'

It was a relief to have someone to talk to about all this, Best thought. He only hoped he wasn't making a mistake about his landlady. She'd hinted that it had been a personal tragedy that had made her feel this way and to write the letters. But she hadn't elaborated and he hadn't pressed her. She would tell him in time.

The *Islington Gazette* was demanding to know why so many of its readers had drowned and was pointing the finger straight at the local vestry. In a parish of nearly a quarter of a million souls there was only one small, private swimming bath, their leader page pointed out furiously. But what had the vestry done, when a public facility had been mooted, following the recent Public Baths and Washhouses Act? Not only had they declined to take advantage, they had resisted the idea 'with something approaching prejudice'! This, while St Pancras, a similar neighbouring area (but with a council less pretentious to refinement and intelligence), had taken up the question with a liberal spirit.

This may have been, the newspaper conceded, partly because that at the same time the idea of free public libraries had been suggested. But now the library notion had been shelved, they should go ahead with vigour.

Ideas for keeping afloat in water continued to pour into the newspapers. They ranged from removable cork seating cushions on all pleasure craft (which seemed to Best quite a sensible idea) to using an open umbrella or the rim of one's hat to support one. The notion that ladies, too, should learn to swim, had also gained ground particularly since, it was reported, that only one lady had been able to save herself in this manner. Women's multi-layered clothes, it was also conceded, were probably no help with buoyancy.

He intended to take quite a strong line with Helen on learning to swim and he wondered how Murphy must be feeling, given his previous, strident opposition. But, truth to tell, Best knew that even had Martha been able to swim she would have stood little chance of survival given where she had been sitting at the time of impact. Maybe he would find an opportunity to tell Murphy that – if he could find a way which made it sound less horrendous.

The occasional body from the *Princess Alice* was still surfacing, the papers reported. The first part of the inquest was virtually over and a verdict of 'drowned' brought in on the majority of the 623 bodies found. A particularly depressing note was that this number included eleven who had reached the shore alive but died soon afterwards.

Blame for the accident was still being bandied about and no conclusion could be reached until the end of both the second half of the inquest and the Board of Trade enquiry which was now underway. But rumour had it that not only had the pleasure boat's lookout system been pathetically inadequate, but that the man steering the craft had never done so before and, indeed, had only taken over at Gravesend, as a favour for a friend who wanted a night out.

Best laid the papers down. He had realized that he could act with a little more freedom now that Mrs O'Connor was sharing observation duty. And there were another couple of calls he should make.

This time, Best turned right, rather than left, as he came out of 9 John Street. Staying on the sunny side he crossed Thornhill Road and continued on down the hill, past the new North London Synagogue which served the area's German and Polish Jews. He paused to admire its large, white, glass globes perching high on scrolled ironwork supports either side of the decorative entrance gates and the handsome carvings on the porch beyond.

His watch showed 2.30 p.m., his step was light, and his stomach replete with Mrs O'Connor's best pea soup and a portion of pork pie. There were distinct advantages in having her as a co-conspirator. Previously he had had to make do with bread and butter and a little cheese at midday, and that as a concession as her other 'gentlemen' needed to be fed only in the evening.

He continued across Hemingford Road lined with flat-roofed terraced houses and large, semi-detached villas, iced with much white paintwork giving them a decidedly Hansel and Gretel air. On, down through Thornhill Square – which wasn't square at all but pear-shaped, with the fatter end being sliced off by John Street. Sitting squat in the centre of the resultant crescent was the cream-coloured, large and lumpy St Andrew's Church. It would have looked fine on the breast of a wild Scottish moorland, Best felt, but was somewhat overwhelming in this dignified, residential neighbourhood.

He was in familiar country. Best had trodden these streets and squares as a young constable, posted to N division. Indeed, he had been here when some of the more recent houses in this ever-burgeoning area were being built. It had been one of his duties to keep a close eye on the piles of bricks and stacks of timber which had a habit of disappearing from one site and reappearing on another. He recalled the camaraderie of those days with affection, but not the endless patrolling and oppressive discipline.

Best reached Caledonian Road, a wide thoroughfare leading north from King's Cross. Further up 'the Cally' brooded the huge Pentonville Prison and, close by, the Royal Caledonian Asylum, an orphanage for the sons of Scots killed on active service – which had given the road its name. He remembered how the kilted uniforms of the boys often brightened these grey streets.

Best dodged between the heavy traffic and began threading his way through the streets beyond. The terraces here were more densely packed than those on the other side of 'the Cally' and the houses meaner. They were dirtier, too, despite being fairly recently built. Soot from the trains, dust from the railway coal depot and local brick and tile works saw to that. It was also smellier down here where the more noxious offshoots of the nearby Metropolitan Cattle Market, such as soap making, bone milling, tripe-stripping and varnish manufacture, had taken root. Not surprisingly the residents, too, were poor and dirty and smelly, unlike those up the hill to the east.

Soon he had reached his destination, Stroud's Vale, an oddly sylvan name, he thought, for an area overlooking the mainline railway into King's Cross.

He found the house he was looking for, rang the bell and waited. There was no response.

'What d'you want, mister?' came a sudden coarse shout from below.

He looked down to the basement area and got the shock of his life. 'Nella!' he exclaimed.

Chapter Eighteen

'Nah!' exclaimed the young girl who stood in the open doorway of the basement with a toddler clutching her skirt. 'I ain't Nella. I'm her sister, Jessie.'

When Best descended the steep steps he saw the difference immediately. Not only was this girl younger, she had a more prominent nose and teeth, and none of her sister's spark. Indeed, her expression was straightforwardly sullen.

'Nella's dead,' she said bluntly.

'I know,' admitted Best. 'It was just that you looked so much like her.'

'Well, she was my sister, wasn't she?' she said doggedly, as though to a simpleton. 'Stands to reason, don't it?'

Best agreed that it did. 'Is your father in?' he enquired, in an effort to end this pointless exchange.

'No, 'course not,' she said suspiciously. 'He's at work, ain't he?' She blocked the doorway making it clear he would not be invited in. Close to, her face was grimy and her clothes limp and dirty. Best was happy not to be invited in, given the glimpse he could see of the filthy interior. 'Who are you, anyway?' she said, sharply.

'I found Nella's body. I knew her slightly because I was living next door in John Street.' Best felt silly being wrongfooted by this child and having to stand on the doorstep explaining himself.

'Oh.' Jessie seemed neither impressed nor curious.

'I helped your father bury her.'

'Oh, yeh.' Jessie shifted her weight on to her other foot and rubbed her back. ' 'E said there was a bloke what did.' The news that Best was the bloke did not soften her.

'I brought these for the children.' He handed over a bag of boiled sweets which she took without thanks. 'I just wanted to see your father to tell him about how I got on with his application to the Lord Mayor's Fund.'

She looked at him blankly although he could have sworn he saw a flicker of interest in her eyes. Best was tired of this.

'Will he be in tomorrow night?'

'Mebbe,' she replied truculently.

'I'll be here at 8.30 p.m.,' he snapped. 'Tell him to be in,' he added bluntly as he turned on his heel and stomped up the steps, his good mood gone.

Best was greeted rather more warmly the following afternoon. Mrs Dawes, if he was not mistaken, had got herself up especially for the occasion. She was wearing a maroon velvet afternoon gown and ropes of pearls which set off her only remaining good point, her peachy-soft fair skin.

It occurred to him that both her attire and the contents of the room, now losing its initial chill as a newly laid fire warmed it, were rather more expensive than what might be expected in this average Islington street – as, apparently, were some of the clientele.

Mrs Dawes must be fifty if she was a day, but, he decided, given the obvious extra effort she'd put in, a little judicious flattery would not go amiss. He complimented her on her gown and she blushed demurely and thanked him. However, he sensed that it was unlikely she would be easily taken in. There was a native knowingness and cunning nestling below those soft cheeks and voluptuous bosom. Indeed, she could well be playing him at his own game. He would have to tread carefully.

After he had duly described the sad demise of Martha – not sparing the ghastly details – she said, 'And how did Martha seem beforehand? Was she happy? I do hope so.'

Best was about to jump in with tales of the young woman's good spirits when he realized that she was awaiting his reply with some expectancy. He hesitated, then swiftly decided that honesty was the best policy. Well, a nod in the direction of honesty anyway. So many of the victims came from Islington, some survivors must do so as well. Possibly, survivors known to Mrs Dawes and Martha and who may have seen her weeping.

'A little upset, I'm sad to say,' he admitted with a shrug and show of reluctance. 'Indeed, that's why I spoke to her when I saw her sitting near the paddle box.'

'She was crying?' asked Mrs Dawes.

Now he knew she knew.

He nodded. 'And since we had acknowledged each other in passing, it seemed churlish not to stop and enquire whether she was all right.'

'Of course. Of course. How kind you are.' She paused. 'And what was it that was troubling her?'

'Well, at first I couldn't make it out, but I guessed it must be something to do with the little chap I'd seen her with at Rosherville.'

'And it was?'

'Yes. Apparently she was sad she'd had to leave him behind. Understandable, really.'

'Of course. And were you able to comfort her?'

'I hope so, a little. But, just as she was drying her eyes there was the commotion up front and I dashed forward ... '

There was a short silence while they gave the moment due solemnity. Then Mrs Dawes leaned forward and patted his hand. 'You comforted her, Mr Best. You can always be glad about that.'

He relaxed a little. He had passed the test. She seemed satisfied. He had managed to bring into play the first principle of a good defence when guilty – admit to known facts but put a different interpretation on them. The strategy had saved many an outright villain and always would.

Tea and small cakes were brought in and Mrs Dawes threw herself into acting the hostess. It wasn't until he had bitten into a delicious coconut macaroon that she threw her second body blow.

'I hear that it was you who found poor Nella's body, Mr Best?'

He had been wondering whether to bring up the other two people concerned: Nella and Murphy. He had no idea how involved Murphy was with this household, but had decided to avoid mentioning him at this stage. The subject of Nella he would broach. After all, her father was known here. Mrs Dawes had beaten him to it, thus putting him at a disadvantage. She was no fool.

He nodded as he swallowed, endeavouring neither to choke nor appear disconcerted. Once his mouth was clear, he admitted as naturally as possible that this was also the case. 'I hesitated to bring it up, dear lady, in case it upset you too much. Two such deaths in one household ... '

'Well, of course, Nella had left. ... '

'Oh yes, I realized that, but also that you would have an affection for her.'

'Indeed, I did.'

'I couldn't believe it when I found her. I wasn't really sure at first. I'd only seen her once or twice when she was pegging out clothes in the garden and she'd stopped for a minute to admire my painting ... but her father confirmed it was the poor child,'

'Such a sad, sad business.'

It was a much more relaxed Mrs Dawes who pressed him to more cakes and enquired whether he painted portraits as well as garden subjects. He made her smile at his description of his struggles just to paint the dog roses, bringing all his charm into play and even treating her to his full, flashing smile. Something he rarely lavished on the English, knowing that some found it over-expressive and 'foreign'.

'You must pop in for tea again,' she pressed him when he complimented her on her hospitality and took his leave.

He certainly would, he declared warmly.

Best had been dying to ask Nella's father pertinent questions about what had happened to her between the time he had last seen her in the garden and her body being found. But, as he was meant to be no more than a casual acquaintance of hers, he had so far desisted. Nor had his colleagues been able to question the man in depth. The fact that she may have been murdered had not yet been revealed.

Berger had told the police that Nella had returned home after the birth but then taken off without warning. Later, he had discovered she had gone for a day trip on the *Princess Alice*. It was a complete mystery to him how or why she had done this and who could have given her the money. It had been a bit of a mystery to Best how she could have felt fit enough to take such an excursion so soon after the birth. In fact, he now knew that she hadn't.

Best was still holding himself back as he sat across from Berger in a room which had obviously seen a little hasty tidying and even the application of the odd wet rag since he had half-glimpsed it the day before. Even the sullen Jessie was making a little effort to be civil under the watchful eye of her father. But she spoke only when prompted by him. Indeed, reacted only to him.

The place was cold and the bare floorboards, softened only by a couple of worn mats, made it feel colder. Berger indicated that they should draw closer to the meagre fire, which was sending what little heat it provided straight up the chimney.

Berger, all sign of mourning gone, was obviously pleased when Best told him that the Lord Mayor's Fund had agreed that he was entitled to more money. But not so happy to learn that he would have to wait until the final inquest verdict before it could be released.

'Vy so?' he asked indignantly. 'Everyone else has got theirs.' As his anger grew, Jessie became very still and tense as she sat in the corner of the room where the three other children lay sleeping under an overcoat. 'Vy I have to vait?' Berger thumped his clenched fist into his other palm. 'You say it is just a formality – but I need food for children!'

And drink to drink, thought Best. He had caught the smell on the man's breath as he came in and was pretty sure that was why Jessie hadn't known whether her father would be in tonight. It was probably only the prospect of money that had tempted him away from the pub.

Best leaned forward and put out his hand which contained a small roll of notes. 'They have kindly authorized me to give you this meanwhile.'

He saw some of the stiffness go out of Jessie's body and heard a small sigh of relief.

Berger was too distracted to notice her reaction. He tried to grab the money but Best stayed his hand, making him count it out and sign a receipt before handing it over.

'I still feel so sad about Nella,' Best murmured when their business was done.

'Yeh. Very sad,' said Berger, shifting restlessly on his chair. It was clear the man did not want to waste drinking time in exchanging polite conversation.

'I've explained your need,' he reminded Berger, 'and that you should have special consideration.'

That regained his attention. 'Good. Good. You have been good help to me.'

'You know, it was so sudden,' said Best.

'The accident. *Ja.*'

'No. Nella's disappearance.'

'Disappearance. Vot disappearance?'

'From John Street.' Best smiled sadly. 'Understandable really. Their time comes. They have their baby and they go.'

'*Ja*. That's how it is.'

'Just wasn't able to say goodbye, I suppose.'

Berger seemed uncertain of how to react to Best's amiable ramblings. '*Ja*,' he mumbled.

Best leaned forward, concerned. 'Tell me, did she have an easy time?'

'Easy? Vot … ?'

'The birth. I hope it wasn't too difficult for her. The poor girl was long overdue – she told me.'

Berger sat back, relieved. 'Oh, no.' He shrugged. 'It vos easy. Very easy, they told me.' He laughed. 'Been vaiting so long to come out, I guess.'

Best smiled in a comradely way. Poor, bloody Nella with a father like this. The tears at the burial, he now realized, were either for himself or just for show. Or an amalgam of both.

'Was it a boy or a girl?' Best longed to be out of this stinking hole but persisted with his seemingly rambling enquiries about a girl he'd only met in passing and formed a certain fondness for.

'Oh. A boy.' Berger spread out his wide square hands. 'A big boy.'

Best sighed. 'I wish I'd seen him.' He smiled. 'Was he like his mother?'

'Oh *ja. Ja*,' said Berger, then proudly, 'and a bit like me!' He laughed. Then he pulled himself up. 'His grandfather.'

'I hope he found a good home.'

'Oh *ja. Ja*. Always, with Mrs Dawes. Rich people. Very rich.'

'Good. Nella seemed pleased about that. Giving the baby the best chance in life.' He paused before continuing.

'Would you know who they are? I mean, if I wanted to give the child a christening present … ' he enquired vaguely. 'I did tell Nella I would, but … '

Berger shook his head. 'We not know. Better that way.'

Best sighed. 'Yes, I suppose you're right.'

He'd asked enough questions – none of which had got him very far but had, he hoped, seemed innocuous enough. More next time.

It had now been established that Nella had died from suffocation but that there had been no water in her lungs – so she had not drowned. It followed that she had not died in the *Princess Alice* tragedy. Best was determined to find out how and why she did die.

'Look, I'll have another try for some more money from the fund to help keep you going and I'll come back in a couple of nights to tell you how I got on.'

That recaptured his attention – and a certain amount of suspicion.

'You are very good … '

Best shrugged. 'I've nothing else to do till I'm well. It's the least I can do for poor Nella's family.'

To Best's surprise, when he sat down to supper that evening, Murphy was present – looking a thinner and paler version of his usually robust self. So much for his holiday in Ireland. But then, what ailed him was not to be cured by rest, good food and fresh air.

One thing had changed: he was no longer quite so tongue-tied, at least not with Best, whom he continued to treat as his bosom pal.

After supper, they strolled out into the garden for a smoke. The threat of rain hung in the air but it was not cold and the soft evening light was like a balm. Best enquired gently as to how Murphy was bearing up and said, again, how sorry he was about Martha. The Irishman proved eager to talk about her and soon explained something which had long puzzled Best. That was how they had managed to get to know each other, given Murphy's lack of social skill and the fact that there was no obvious contact between the two houses.

'She tripped one day as she was coming down the steps carrying a bundle. I was passing and helped her up. I was going her way, so I carried it for her as far as Upper Street.' He paused then, with a sad man-to-man smile, before confiding, 'I wasn't really going that way you understand. I just pretended that I was.'

His pride in making the most of such an opportunity was touching, but the idea of him carrying the bundle struck Best as decidedly droll. What, he wondered, would such a good Catholic lad, who always said his grace before meals, have thought had he realized that he might well have been carrying a dead baby? It beggared belief, as Mrs O'Connor would say.

'She was upset about not being able to see her boy and I was missing my family back home,' he explained, 'and we got talking.' It was surprising that the inadequate Murphy had been able to do that but, on the other hand, maybe he was better with women. Some men were.

'And so you managed to see her again?' prompted Best.

Murphy nodded, pushing his huge freckled hand through his coarse ginger curls. 'It wasn't easy, you know. She didn't get much time off.' He stopped and gave a small smile which made his simple face more boyish and appealing. 'I did take her to see the Mohawk Minstrels at the Aggy once and another time to Collins's Music Hall - she loved that. She did laugh so much at the minstrels.' A sudden sob came into his throat and Best patted his arm.

Two of the lady 'guests' were sitting near the end of next door's garden. One was knitting, the other reading a book, both were heavily pregnant. As the two men approached they had concentrated even harder on their preoccupations. Not only due to the failing light, Best guessed; they were here incognito, and very likely in disgrace, but when Murphy sobbed, the knitter glanced up in surprise.

Best nodded to her. 'Good evening, ladies.' He glanced up at the sky. 'The light will be catching you out soon, I'm afraid.'

The knitter nodded and smiled back gratefully. 'Yes, I think you're right.' She finished her line, wound up her ball of wool and stuck it on the end of her needles. 'Time to go in, Margaret.' The other woman sighed, closed her book and began heaving herself to her feet. Best would have liked to stay and chat a little, but who knew just who might be noting his interest?

He nodded again to the ladies before turning his attention back to Murphy. 'Sad about Nella,' he said. 'I got such a shock when I found her body.'

Murphy did not reply for a moment, then eventually muttered, 'Yes, I suppose it was sad.'

'Such a young girl.'

Silence.

'You didn't like her?'

'She was a bitch!' he exclaimed suddenly. 'Just a bitch!'

Best was startled by the venom in his voice.

'She was spreading terrible, wild rumours about the house – and about Martha! I could have killed her!'

Oh, thought Best, good grief. That's something I didn't reckon on. But did you, Mr Murphy, that's the question? Did you?

Somehow he didn't think so.

Chapter Nineteen

Voices were raised. Male voices. Best strained to catch what they were saying. It seemed to him he heard the exclamation, 'dangerous!' then lower angry mumbling out of which he picked 'pregnant' and 'no use now!'. In the background a woman was crying.

'All Islington has been in mourning, Mr Best,' Mrs Dawes's lisping, pseudo-genteel voice was raised deliberately to drown out the invading sound.

'Tch tch, what a dreadful noise,' she exclaimed when she could ignore it no longer. 'I expect it's that butcher, Jones, disputing the bill again.' She sighed. 'These tradesmen.'

She picked up a small silver bell from the occasional table and shook it vigorously. Despite her efforts Best doubted its tinkling sound would carry far but, to his surprise, there was a tap on the door quite quickly and the skivvy appeared around it. 'Mary,' said Mrs Dawes irritably, 'do tell whoever is making that dreadful noise to desist immediately!'

The girl looked confused.

'Tell them to stop at once! We have an important guest in here!'

'Yes, Mrs Dawes.' In fact, the voices had now grown more distant.

It was interesting, thought Best, that she hadn't enquired who was making the noise. There couldn't be that many possibilities and he was sure the local butcher was not one of them.

'Oh, and do bring some fresh tea. And, Mary' – she stopped the girl as she was leaving – 'if Dr Helman is still about ask him to pop in here, will you?'

'Yes, ma'am.'

'He comes in to examine our lady guests,' she explained to Best. 'I expect you've heard about the service we provide here.'

My God. That was one way of putting it but he was surprised she had mentioned it at all. 'Yes,' he admitted. 'I've seen some of your lady guests in the garden so I gathered this was a lying-in establishment.'

'We like to call it a clinic,' she simpered. 'We offer the best of care to ladies in confinement.'

Today, she was wearing a low-cut, black moire dress which made her look more like a plump pouter pigeon than ever. Judging by her ever-changing wardrobe and accompanying jewellery, care in confinement seemed to pay well. This, Best thought, is a far cry from the poverty-stricken, ill-fated Mrs Waters and her filthy establishment.

He didn't quite know what was expected of him next so he smiled and said, 'When I first saw the ladies I was a little fearful, I admit.'

She frowned and grew still. 'Fearful, Mr Best?'

'Yes, I imagined being kept awake at night by squalling babies! But I have not heard any crying. You must have a magic touch with them.' Even to Best himself that sounded just a little too sugary but she simpered and laughed, causing her ample creamy bosom to rise and fall repeatedly. He wondered whether he was being reckless, bringing up the subject of the non-crying babies, but she didn't seem disturbed.

'That, Mr Best, is because the babies don't stay. We have such a list of eager adopters awaiting them. People able to give them a fine upbringing and a good life.'

'So Mr Berger tells me. He speaks very highly of your service.'

'And well he might. We found his granddaughter some splendid adopters.'

Granddaughter? Best had scarcely digested this information when there was a rap on the door and, without waiting for a reply, a tall, dark man entered, wearing a black frock coat and striped trousers. It was the same person he had seen arguing with Martha in the garden – what now seemed an eternity ago. 'Dr Helman,' Mrs Dawes simpered. 'This is Mr Best. The gentleman I was telling you about – the last person to see Martha alive, poor dear.' She paused. 'And, alas, also found Nella's body.' As she spoke, Helman came towards Best, holding out his hand. 'I knew you would like to meet him.'

'Of course. Of course.' The doctor's voice lacked enthusiasm.

Why, thought Best? Were they still frightened Martha had told him something?

'Such a bad business. We were devastated.' The man's fleshy hand grasped his and he placed the other one over the top and held it there as he shook it. Helman had a rich, whisky voice and breath to match. Clearly he had once been handsome, but now he was puffy around the eyes and his clothes had a slightly careless look about them. Not exactly gone to seed but well on the way, thought Best.

'Oh, you must have been,' said Best. 'They seemed such pleasant young women although I admit to only the most fleeting acquaintance with them.' Good grief, he was speaking like Mrs Dawes now. Like someone out of Jane Austen!

'Do stay for some tea, Doctor,' she said patting the couch beside her.

'Well, I'm not certain I have the time … '

'He's such a busy man,' said Mrs Dawes to Best. She patted the seat again, this time in a more commanding manner. A timid knock on the door signalled the arrival of fresh tea. The doctor acquiesced and sat down.

Best was still puzzled as to why Mrs Dawes had wanted Helman to meet him. Was she still suspicious? Did she want a second opinion? Or was she making sure that he knew that Helman was part of this set up? If so, why? He was still musing on this matter as the door opened. He looked up expecting to see Mary again.

'Jessie!' he exclaimed, at the sight of the nervous young woman holding the tray.

'I couldn't help myself,' Best told Mrs O'Connor later. 'It was such a surprise.'

'And you supposed to be a professional dissembler, Mr Best. Shame on you!' She shook her head in disbelief. 'Isn't it just as well they already knew about your acquaintance with the family?'

He grimaced self-deprecatingly and nodded. 'Mrs Dawes explained afterwards that she needed more help and Jessie was filling in till her time came.'

'Oh, dear God, another one.'

'I'm afraid so.'

'It'll be that father of hers.'

Best was startled. 'That's what Helen said about Nella.'

'Well now, it's a common enough thing. I can't see why you're surprised.'

'We don't know for sure, do we?'

'Huh,' she replied and raised her eyebrows. 'It seems to me there is surely a possibility there.'

'But it wasn't just that,' he confessed. 'What I couldn't understand was, why had she asked me to tea again so quickly and why she brought Helman in to meet me?'

Mrs O'Connor smiled to herself. 'I think maybe I can.'

'You?' Best was startled. He gazed at his Cheshire cat landlady. 'What on earth do you mean?'

'Well, it's like this. I was thinking that things needed hurrying along a little and that you'd been telling me I should make friends with those monsters next door.'

'Yes … '

'So, I did make an effort in spite of my reservations.'

'Mrs O'Connor,' begged Best. But she was not to be hurried.

'When that woman came out into the garden the other day to speak to some of her "ladies", I popped my head over the fence and offered my condolences.'

She paused. 'It was the least I could do, don't you think?'

Best was sitting on the edge of his chair. 'Mrs O'Connor!'

She looked at him pityingly and continued, 'Well, naturally, didn't that lead on to you, and your involvement in the matter. Then to your position in life – we chatted quite a while, you understand.'

'Position in life?' Best was becoming alarmed.

'Financial position, we're talking about here. You know,' she said as though explaining to a slow-witted child, 'you being a wealthy man and all, and liking to invest in small propositions with quick returns.'

He gazed at her open-mouthed. 'What!' he exclaimed half-laughing. He contemplated her with astonishment for a moment, his mind racing to grasp what she was saying. 'Ah, but there's a flaw in your story, Mrs O'Connor,' he said eventually.

'Is that right, young man?'

'If I am wealthy, why am I living here?' He looked around, 'Comfortable as it is.'

'Ah, that would be because you're keeping your head down. That little business you were involved in, in the City. Mightn't the authorities be glad to know where you are?'

He gazed at her with astonishment. 'So, that means if I don't cough up something for their establishment … '

'And you're very likely to – given that you're a bit silly about money,' she assured him. 'Think you know a lot, you understand, but sure, you don't really. That's why I'm able to fiddle you on the rent.'

Best could hardly speak for laughing. 'So, if I don't cough up, even though I'm a bit silly about money – they could "persuade" me.'

'Well now, that's about it, yes,' she admitted, then sat back and folded her arms across her chest in a confident, housewifely fashion.

When Best had stopped laughing he asked, 'Why didn't you tell me all this beforehand? So I could be prepared?'

She contemplated him with wonder. 'But then you wouldn't have acted so natural, now would you?'

Best, not usually at a loss for words, was, for once, struck dumb.

Cheadle and Smith were similarly affected when he described his landlady's actions.

'I think we could do with this woman in the department,' chuckled Cheadle, who at first had been angry on learning that Best had revealed his identity to her.

'I've been thinking what I can do with this opportunity,' said Best when they had quietened down. 'I can ask to inspect the premises.'

'And get to talk to the domestics,' interrupted Cheadle. In his estimation the key to all crime puzzles lay with the domestics.

'I doubt whether I'll get much from Jessie,' Best warned.

'Oh, but you've got to,' insisted Cheadle. 'She'll know what happened to her sister. Use your charm,' he said, not quite as sarcastically as usual. The man is softening, thought Best, no doubt about it.

'And I'll talk to some of the lady guests and, of course, in depth to Mrs Dawes, particularly about what happens to the babies.'

'What you going to do about the money?' asked Cheadle bluntly. 'Did this smart landlady of yours tell you where that was coming from?'

'Well ... '

'The commissioner won't give you none, I'll tell you that.'

'I thought I would tell them my funds are tied up for a few weeks.'

'They won't buy that for long.'

'I know. But I'm sure it'll work for a while. After all, it's them coming to me. I never said I had any ready money, did I?' He paused and took a deep breath. 'But if it becomes vital that I produce something quickly, I do have a promise of some help.'

Cheadle sat up abruptly, 'From this landlady?'

'Yes; Mrs O'Connor has offered to put in a little – a hundred or two – her savings – to keep things going.'

'What's her game?'

'She wants it stopped.'

'Hmm.' Cheadle looked suspicious.

'She's a good lady,' insisted Best.

'When you say, "put in", she realizes—?'

'That she might not get it back? Yes.'

There was a short silence.

'There's no alternative, is there?' Best asked eventually.

Another silence as Cheadle pulled at the ends of his once luxurious moustache, now showing signs of thinning. He sank lower in his chair as he brooded. 'Don't like civvies getting involved.'

Best didn't say anything.

'All right. All right,' the chief inspector agreed eventually. 'I'll 'ave to tell the chief superintendent and Mr Vincent. Who knows, they might be able to get the commissioner to cough up some funds to 'elp the department get back on its feet. Though 'eaven 'elp you if it all goes wrong and you lose it.'

Thanks, thought Best. The usual, gracious support.

'Where's Joseph?' asked Best, expecting Helen to say upstairs or out in the park with Mrs Briggs.

'With Matilda.'

Matilda was Helen's younger sister who had caused them such grief when she had run off with the young Van Ellen.

They'd thought she might have been murdered. Best had been given the job of finding her and that had brought him and Helen together.

'What time will he be back?' Best shouldn't really be visiting Helen but he was snatching an hour after his Yard visit. But he dared not be away from John Street too long. Mrs O'Connor couldn't be on constant watch and, anyway, there wasn't much she could do if something happened. Thank goodness Cheadle had agreed to Smith coming in for short periods.

'He won't be back.'

Best stopped in the act of removing his soaking wet topcoat and frowned. 'What d'you mean?'

'He's staying with them for the moment.'

'Why?'

'Because there are other children there to keep him company and because they are happy to take him.' She paused. 'It could be the answer to our problem.'

'What problem?'

'What to do about Joseph.'

'That's not a problem.'

'Not to you, perhaps! Mrs Briggs has done her best but she's not been well and I have my living to earn!'

This was their first row. She was wearing that stupid shapeless green dress again, he noticed irritably. The woman had no style!

He dragged off the rest of his sodden coat and hung it on the hall coat rack. 'You have no right to make decisions about Joseph without consulting me.'

'You weren't here!' she flung back. 'And I had no idea when you would be back!'

Best removed his bowler and vainly tried to mop the wet from it with his handkerchief, but ended up looking helplessly at his wet hands and wondering where to dry them.

Helen stomped off into the kitchen and returned with a towel which she pushed into his hands.

'I'll go and see him in St John's Wood,' he said gruffly.

'You can't.'

'Why not?'

'Because they've gone down to Boxmere for a few days.'

Boxmere was their country house in Buckinghamshire. Best gritted his teeth and got on with drying himself, rubbing angrily at his wet face, hair and hands. The woman could be dreadful. How had he ever become involved with her? He knew some thought the attraction was that she was more educated and of a higher class than he, but it was more likely she'd caught him when he was still grieving over Emma – whom she could never replace.

'I don't suppose you asked Joseph how he feels about this,' he snapped.

'Yes, I did, and he was pleased. He wanted to go!'

Best glared at her. If he was, it must have been due to her coldness, poor boy.

'Little Edward is his best friend – ever – he says.' She softened a little. 'You should see them together. It's done him the world of good.'

Best refused to be convinced or to give way.

The corners of Helen's mouth began to twitch.

'What are you smirking at?' Even he realized that sounded pretty rude but she began to laugh.

'You look so funny, Inspector Best, standing there all indignant, with your hair sticking out in all directions and your face all red.'

He glanced in the hallstand mirror. She was right. He looked bloody ridiculous. Her now impishly smiling face appeared behind him in the mirror and his heart lurched. She was such a beguiling woman, so different from any other he'd known – that was why he loved her so.

Chapter Twenty

Jessie, taking in next door's wash in the late evening sun, was a sight which unnerved Best. From where he was standing she looked so much like Nella – though not yet so pregnant – it was almost as though time had stood still. He wished it had.

But then, he told himself before he became too melancholy (a previously alien trait), you have another chance with this one. You can save her. Maybe he was being dramatic. She might not be in any danger. Well, at least he could help and comfort her. If she'd let him.

Since seeing the washing hung out he had been waiting in the garden for a long time in the hope that Jessie would come to collect it. By the time she did, he'd had to give up the pretence of painting, due to the fading light. Instead, he resorted to contemplative smoking and desultory squinting at the *Islington Gazette*, which didn't cheer him much. Two more tiny bodies had been found locally, more elsewhere which, of course, brought reiteration of the cry that something must be done about it. He wondered whether they were wasting their time trying to stem the flow from this source when there seemed to be so many.

Maybe Helen was right when she had said child-dropping would only cease when birth control was fully accepted; men were forced to pay a decent amount to help raise their illegitimate children and the affiliation orders were made to work. He became embarrassed when she talked about birth control. It was not a proper subject for a lady.

Whatever the ifs and buts, there was still poor Nella's death to avenge.

Jessie ignored him and he pretended that he hadn't seen her. But, as she worked her way down the line towards him, unpegging, folding and placing the clothes and sheets neatly in the basket, he raised his voice and without looking up said, 'I used to talk to your sister when she was doing that.'

There was no reply. He hadn't expected any. 'Of course she was much more pregnant than you.' Again no reply, but out of the corner of his eye he saw her hesitate as she pulled out a peg. He turned his head as she came close. She looked pale and frightened. Suddenly he jumped to his feet and strolled across to the fence. He'd established that Mrs Dawes was not suspicious of him, indeed she had been persuaded that he was a bit of an ass, so he took the chance. 'When we first met I heard this strange sound coming from just there.' He pointed to the spot just below where he stood. 'So, I came over to see what it was.' He hesitated and saw Jessie stop mid-fold. 'It turned out to be Nella – and she was weeping.'

The girl's hand trembled as she removed the next peg. Eventually, she looked at him and said, 'What for?' Her voice broke and her face began to crumble. 'Why was she crying?' she managed.

To his alarm he realized Jessie was near to tears. He wanted to make contact and was using wiles to do so but he'd gone too far. This could ruin it. He adopted a more cheerful conciliatory tone; 'Oh, it was about having to give her baby away. But she soon cheered up after we'd chatted about it going to a good home and having a better life than she could give it.'

It was the best he could do but it didn't work. Her shoulders hunched over and she began to sob piteously. Best glanced anxiously at the darkening windows of the house. They told him nothing. Thank goodness she'd reached the end of that clothes-line.

'Quick,' he commanded. 'Go to the next line so the sheets hide you! Come on – stand up straight and go!'

She struggled to stand upright and stumbled across the rough grass to reach the sanctuary of the next line of washing. 'We don't want anyone to see you crying!' Best insisted.

He raised his voice again. 'Keep working,' he instructed. 'And don't worry. I'm going to help you. And, if anyone asks what I was talking to you about, say I was just saying it was a nice evening and chatting to you about your sister. All right?' There was no reply, only muffled, choking sounds.

'All right?' he insisted.

'Ye–s,' came the word hesitantly.

'Stop that crying,' he ordered as though to a child, which was all she was really, 'and keep unpegging that washing. Wipe your eyes on your sleeve. But if they notice your eyes are red, say you were thinking about Nella, right? And missing her.'

Another muffled, 'Ye–s.' The line swung backwards and forwards erratically as she made clumsy efforts to unpeg. 'I'll speak to you again,' he assured her. 'Don't worry. Everything will be all right.'

He wished he could be as sure as he sounded.

'We have several bedrooms,' explained Mrs Dawes, 'which of course vary according to what our ladies can afford.'

Best had noticed how bleak and bare some rooms were compared with others more warmly furnished and decorated. Even down to the last detail. The better ones had splendid oil lamps, the poorer had candle stumps in pottery holders. He reckoned there were six rooms in all. Not a lot.

'I can get three in here,' said Mrs Dawes, opening the door to a room fit to house only one non-pregnant person.

'A bit of a squeeze but some of them are used to that at home or in the servants' quarters!' She laughed. She was probably right, there. 'Of course, clients for these cheaper rooms tend to come in later so there is a quick turnover,' she confided with some satisfaction. One fair-haired, rather wan girl was lying on the bed looking rather poorly. The room was chilly and there was no fire in the grate.

'Don't forget your duties, Jane,' said Mrs Dawes crisply. Which answered his question as to how such ladies afforded the fees. Some of it paid in kind. 'A few odd jobs, you understand.'

He understood all right.

'They get so lazy, just lying about,' Mrs Dawes complained, as she was shutting the door.

'Do you have to have a licence?' asked Best, who was endeavouring to appear a novice on the subject. 'Wasn't there a law … ?'

'Oh no,' she replied firmly. 'That's only for baby-farmers. We don't keep the babies so it's not necessary.' So much for the new Infant Life Protection Act – it only protected the still living.

Best tried to smile as he looked down at Mrs Dawes who was standing very close to him. 'That must be a relief, no interference from the authorities.' He sighed as though he knew what that entailed.

'Oh, how true.' She touched his arm sympathetically. 'Not that we have anything to hide, of course.'

'I'm sure not,' he agreed. 'This looks to me like a very well-run establishment. Unlikely to attract police attention,' he said hopefully.

She touched his arm again and looked up at him, 'And one very worthwhile investing in,' she assured him. 'Quick return, too.' She dimpled at her little joke.

Jessie appeared beside them, coughed and said timidly, 'Mrs Dawes – there's a lady making henquiries.'

'Show her into the drawing-room.'

'I 'ave but she's in an 'urry. Says she can't wait long.'

'Tch. Tch. Just as our little tour was proceeding so well.'

'Mrs Dawes, don't lose a customer,' exclaimed Best. 'I can come back tomorrow. I don't live very far away, do I?'

'Of course!' As she laughed in response, her powdered bosom rose and fell. 'We can have another *tête-à-tête*. I look forward to that.'

Best cursed inwardly at the interruption. He was just about to enquire about the strategies she used to find adopters so as to get her to make claims which he could later disprove. He would have to launch into the subject cold next time. Which was never so easy.

'What about that little errand?' Mrs Dawes said to Jessie as they descended the stairs.

'I was just going, Mrs Dawes, when the lady come.' And, indeed, she was wearing her little brown wool hat and shawl.

'Get along with you then.'

'Yes, Mrs Dawes.'

It seemed the arrival of this 'lady' had disrupted the plans of others as well. As Best passed the drawing-room door he glanced in crossly to catch a glimpse of the woman Mrs Dawes was greeting. As he did so he nearly died of shock. He couldn't believe his eyes. It was a blessing that Mrs Dawes had her back to him and Jessie had already left.

What in God's name was going on! Why had Helen come here! She couldn't be pregnant. Could she? The very idea rocked him to his core. Why not, he finally asked himself? What did he know about what she had been doing in Paris? The French were so much more casual about these matters – and wasn't it she who had defended places like these? But, no. It was impossible. Unbelievable! But the more he thought about it the more he realized that it was possible. Helen enjoyed defying convention. He was sick at heart.

Jessie had turned left as she left the house, then, at the last moment, she turned left again into Liverpool Road. His heart sank even more when he realized she was carrying a bundle. He must follow, mind whirling, doubts assailing him, being dismissed then arising again.

Think straight, man, think straight, he admonished himself. What other reason could Helen have for being there? Enquiring for a friend? But who? And surely she wouldn't really countenance such a place?

But hadn't she said they were inevitable? Gone on about women being dragged down by the number of children they had to bear? Not her sister, surely. They had money enough. But would she come to a place right next door to where Best was keeping watch? Was she trying to taunt him? Then a sickening thought struck him: he had never told her the address, not even the exact whereabouts of the house.

Jessie's step was quickening but he still managed to keep her woolly bobble in view amongst the other pedestrians. But then, suddenly, the bobble was gone.

He looked around desperately. Oh no, he'd been too eager to keep his distance and, let's face it, too preoccupied. He was going to mess it up again! Then, as the tram in front moved along, he spied her in the middle of the road waiting for a space in the traffic to complete her crossing.

He crossed further up and, this time, once she'd made it to the other side, closed the gap between them. Putting the business of Helen to the back of his mind and concentrating on his quarry was difficult. She'd said they should hurry things up. That was it. She was trying to help him with his investigation, getting inside information. That brought him inexorably back to the fact that she didn't know the whereabouts of the suspect house.

Jessie had passed the first row of the Laycock Farm cattle lairs when suddenly she turned down, into Laycock Yard, and continued alongside more pens. Then she glanced around furtively, causing Best to duck behind a parked cart.

When he emerged, she had gone.

He hurried forward in time to catch sight of her walking between the stables and workshops of the London General Omnibus Manufactory. What was she doing there? Not, he hoped, what he suspected. If so, what on earth was he going to do in response?

Chapter Twenty-One

'Hello Jessie,' said Best, as the nervous young girl emerged from the stables. 'What have you been doing?'

She started and looked up at him with fright in her eyes as though caught red-handed doing something very wrong. Then the old Jessie resurfaced.

'Nuffink,' she said defiantly. 'I ain't been doing nuffink!'

'Then why were you in there?' He glanced over her, into the stable. 'Let's have a look, shall we?' He took her arm and tried to guide her back in but she resisted.

'T'ain't no business of yours but if you really want to know I was taken short,' she said sulkily. 'I 'ad to go. Couldn't 'elp it.'

Best shook his head and began exerting some pressure on her arm. 'I don't think that's true, Jessie, do you?'

'Yes, it is!' She was near to tears now but she stared him out. 'Anyway, 'ow do you know?'

'I know because when you went in you were carrying a bundle. Now, you're not.'

She began to tremble. 'Oh Gawd!' she exclaimed, tears spilling over. 'Oh Gawd! They'll 'ang me!'

'Have you killed anyone?' he asked sharply.

'No! No!'

'Well then, they won't hang you.' He knew that was not necessarily so. They'd hanged Mrs Waters without proving she had even meant to do the babies harm and only at the last minute had they commuted the death sentence on her sister – whom some felt was more blameworthy. 'But, if

I'm right about what's in that bundle, this is very serious. You're what's called an accessory after the fact! So you'd better start telling me the truth!'

She began to wail loudly. 'I 'ad to do what she said! I couldn't 'elp it. I didn't do no wrong.'

Best looked around nervously to check whether the noise had attracted any attention from the workshop. So far, no sign. He pushed her into the empty stable.

At first he could see nothing but as his eyes became accustomed to the semi-darkness he spotted a lumpiness in the straw in the right-hand corner.

She was trying to pull away now and threatening to become hysterical. He held on tightly and dragged her over to the tell tale mound where he pushed aside the straw. There it was – the pathetic, naked corpse of a newborn baby boy.

'Mrs Dawes said I 'ad to take the shawl back,' she whined piteously and began to struggle more desperately.

'Shut up!' he commanded sharply. 'Just shut up while I decide what to do with you.'

Right from the start he had been hoping to see what he had just witnessed – someone dumping a baby's body. But, had Mrs Dawes wanted to place him in an appalling quandary she couldn't have managed it better. He didn't want to see this young girl suffering years of hard labour in prison, or worse, the death penalty. Besides, as things stood, she would be much more use to him inside 7 John Street, helping him solve a more serious murder – that of her sister, Nella.

On the other hand, he had found a body. As a police officer he had no choice but to act on that fact. Call other authorities, arrest the girl, charge her …

Jessie had given up her noisy protestations and was whimpering quietly in a corner. She was a pathetic sight. Her pregnancy was becoming more apparent in the thickening waist and expanding curve of her stomach. She was wide-eyed, pale and shivering due not only to fright but also the inadequacy of her thin cotton dress and worn woollen shawl. No wonder she had also wrapped the shawl which had held the baby over the top of her own.

'All right,' he said eventually. 'Pull yourself together and let's go.'

He'd made a decision, right or wrong. He would probably regret it bitterly but somehow he was past caring.

'So who is the father of your baby?'

Jessie looked sullen but Best had the upper hand now.

'The boy next door,' she offered unconvincingly.

'You're lying!' snapped Best. 'I'm risking a lot to help you and you're still lying to me.'

He had given tuppence to a small boy to take an anonymous message to the nearest policeman or police station, telling them the whereabouts of the latest small corpse. He was still in a terrible quandary about what to do next.

While he'd seen Jessie deposit the body he had not yet arrested her – despite the fact that this was the breakthrough they had been awaiting for so long. Cheadle's reaction didn't bear contemplation. That long-awaited promotion would be rescinded and it would be back to the beat – if he was lucky. But more like the sack – or even prison – particularly if the baby had clearly been murdered.

But if he hadn't done his duty in that respect he was determined to make use of his hold over Jessie to extract the truth from her.

'It was your father, wasn't it?'

She froze, struggled to open her mouth to speak, but nothing came out. She was clearly terrified of her father, but even more so at the prospect of being hanged.

Now, they were sitting on a bench in a small green square, tucked away between Upper Street and Liverpool Road. It was getting late but, ironically, light from the back of Miss Andrews Baby Linen Warehouse still caught the sparkling cascades of the small fountain beside them.

'Yeh,' she said eventually, 'it was my father.'

'And Nella's?'

'Yeh.' She hung her head.

But Best wasn't going to let up. He couldn't. 'Who killed Nella?' he demanded.

''Ow should I know!'

'I think you must have some idea.'

'Well, I don't!'

'I'm warning you, I'll take you straight to the police station.'

She was quiet for a moment before adding sadly, 'Look, mister, if I did know I would kill them meself!'

'Could it have been your father?'

She shrugged and looked away. 'Dunno. Can't see why 'e would. She did all the work.'

'I never said he did. I was just asking.'

She grimaced, then admitted, ''E was awful cross with 'er 'cos the baby wouldn't come.' Best shook his head in wonder. 'Said it made things difficult for 'im with Mrs Dawes.'

'But he wouldn't have killed her, surely?'

'Nah, but – well, might not have meant to, like.'

'He beat her?'

'Yeh, always did.'

'But, I mean, this time?'

'Well' – she looked away to hide her tears – 'she said he punched her in the stomach to try to make it come.'

While trying to shut the vision from his mind of poor Nella being beaten, the prospects on his career of the result of his latest action made a poor substitute.

With Jessie's help, he worked out that she had seen Nella only once after he had spoken to her in the garden, all that time ago.

'Yeh, she did seem scared,' Jessie agreed.

'Who of? Apart from your dear father?'

'I ... I dunno.' She shifted, uncomfortably.

'Come on ... '

Silence.

'You have to tell me, Jessie.' Best had softened his voice now, to the gently persuasive.

'Mister, I'm scared.' She took a deep breath.

'When I got there that last time,' she said eventually, 'I was on a message for me dad – Martha and that big fella was 'avin' a go at her.'

'Which big fella? The doctor?'

'Nah. 'Im from next door. The Irish fella.'

'Murphy? Why would he be angry at Nella?'

'I dunno.'

'Was he hitting her?'

'Nah. They was just giving her a piece of their minds, telling her off about something, you know. They was real cross, I'll tell you that. 'E was shouting.'

He sighed. All this was going on while he was sitting painting those stupid dog-roses.

'Look, Jessie,' he said firmly. 'I want you to find out more about what happens to those babies.'

She looked almost relieved. 'Then you won't tell on me?'

'Not if I can help it. Look, don't worry, we'll sort something out.' Oh, will we? he thought. 'Just you keep your eyes open. Is one of the women there about to give birth?'

'Yeh, that Mary Coggins.'

'Right, try and be there. And, Jessie—'

She had jumped up, about to run. 'I got to go,' she said desperately, 'she'll wonder where—'

'—find out what happened to Nella. The other servants will know. And I'll meet you here in the morning, about eleven.'

She looked terrified.

'Be careful. If anything happens – I'm only next door. All right?'

She looked back briefly, nodded, and was gone.

He was torn with doubts. Perhaps he shouldn't be sending her in again. It could be so dangerous. Was it time to stop all this now and just go in, mob-handed? But, surely, this was giving Jessie a chance to keep out of prison? Wasn't it?

Best looked after her with tears in his eyes. The gas lamps were just being lit and their glow enlivened the gathering gloom with cheery spots of light. He sat for a long time as the darkness closed around him until, eventually, the damp chill and the necessity of his appearance at Mrs O'Connor's supper-table persuaded him to get up and make his reluctant way back to John Street.

'What on earth do you mean, you were helping me!' Best exclaimed furiously.

'You seemed to be bogged down.' Although defiant, Helen took a step back as though to retreat from his anger.

'Do I interfere with your painting?'

'No. But,' she hesitated, before continuing stubbornly 'it's not the same thing. Detection involves the human element and common sense. Anyway,' she added bravely in the face of his vehement glare, 'this is women's business. They're the ones left to deal with all the consequences of unwanted pregnancies – so don't be surprised if they take an interest in such matters.'

That John Stuart Mills had a lot to answer for, he thought sourly. *The Subjection of Women* indeed! Men more like! Now they were even wanting the vote!

The glowering and glaring competition was getting them nowhere. Both sat down on her sofa and stared moodily into the distance.

'It might interest you to know,' Best muttered eventually, 'that I was just about to extract some vital information from that woman – before your appearance put an end to our meeting!'

'What information?'

'How she claims to attract adopters so I could refute—'

'Oh, that,' said Helen crisply. 'She says she advertises for them in local London papers but not in that area.'

Best restrained himself for a moment then snapped, 'You'll go to court and repeat that?'

'Of course.'

Best fought the urge to smack her. He didn't want her in court. The whole business seemed to be spiralling out of his control – due to the interference of women. First, Mrs O'Connor, now, Helen. At least Mrs O'Connor hadn't got him in such a state.

They reverted to being sulky, sullen mutes until Best broke the silence by muttering quietly, 'When I saw you there it was a terrible shock. I had no idea why you'd come.'

'Oh,' she murmured knowingly, '*that's* what this is all about.' She smiled. 'You thought I might be pregnant?'

'No, of course not!' He blushed in spite of himself. 'I didn't know what to think. I imagined you might be enquiring for someone else but couldn't think who ... I just didn't know! You could have ruined the whole thing!'

'Didn't it occur to you that I might be helping you?'

'Yes. Of course it did,' he admitted more quietly. 'But I knew I'd never told you the address – nor even the exact whereabouts – and I knew Cheadle wouldn't have done.'

She gave him a long, old-fashioned look.

'Smith,' he said. It was a statement, not a question.

She nodded. 'Don't blame him. I wheedled it out of him by stealth. He didn't even know I was doing it.'

'Well, he should have!'

Now she was using detective wiles against them. Well, he sighed inwardly, going to all this trouble at least showed she cared. He was weary of the whole business and sighed again, this time outwardly. He felt miserable.

Suddenly Helen spoke. 'Mrs Briggs has been baking,' she murmured coaxingly. 'Parkin, cherry cakes and Bath buns ... '

He stared at her in wonderment. Baby-farming, murder, poverty, suspicions, anger – and she was talking about ginger parkin and Bath buns! In spite of himself he began to laugh. Helen joined in. Within moments they were hugging each other, rocking backwards and forwards and laughing hysterically.

From where she slept in the domestics' room, up in the eaves of the house, Jessie could hear the sounds of imminent birth. They were not pleasant.

Mary Coggins was screaming as though she was being tortured and was about to die. Jessie had heard enough such noises in the past to know that the girl wasn't necessarily in mortal danger, although you never knew for certain. Her own mother had died in just such circumstances.

But Mr Best had told her she must be on watch at this time so she got up, wrapped her shawl around her shoulders and sat by the bannisters, awaiting the moment when the screaming would reach its highest pitch before subsiding. She would rush in 'to help the girl who was being attacked' and, hopefully catch them, just as the baby was being born.

It took a long time and, despite the din, her head drooped forward and she fell asleep, still clutching the flimsy balustrade. When she awoke with a guilty start there was only silence. She'd missed it! She'd promised Mr Best and she'd missed it! Now she would hang for sure!

Maybe the screaming had only just stopped? Yes, that was it, she thought wildly. She could still dash in 'to help'. She staggered sleepily to her feet, rushed downstairs and reached for the door handle. As it opened it was pulled from her grasp from the inside as Mrs Dawes appeared, carrying a shawl-wrapped bundle. Close behind her was Dr Helman.

Mrs Dawes gasped as she saw Jessie and exclaimed, 'What are you doing here?' She turned to Dr Helman. 'The little witch has been spying on us!'

'Oh no, Mrs Dawes, ma'am!' gasped the terrified Jessie. 'I heard screaming and I thought Mary was being attacked!'

Mrs Dawes hesitated and for a moment it seemed as though she might believe her. Then her eyes narrowed and a look of disbelief crossed the woman's face. 'If she was,' she hissed, 'she would have been dead by now!'

Doctor Helman nodded coldly. 'Her screaming, as you put it, stopped ten minutes ago.'

The pair exchanged glances.

Mrs Dawes was pulling and tucking the shawl tightly, making sure nothing was revealed. If there was a baby in there it would have no chance of breathing.

'You must have realized she was giving birth!' Mrs Dawes exclaimed. 'You knew she was due!'

'Has she had it, then?' asked Jessie, trying to seem eagerly innocent, but clasping her hands together in front of her to stop them shaking. 'Can I see it?'

Mrs Dawes signalled Helman with her eyes.

He shook his head slightly, whereupon she abandoned all pretence and began nodding her head furiously and saying, 'Go on man! Show you're good for something!'

He stiffened and reached for Jessie but she turned and fled down the stairs in terror.

'Don't be stupid!' he yelled, as he lumbered after her. 'You can't get far!'

Chapter Twenty-Two

While Best sat, waiting for Jessie, he contemplated on what had happened so far, wondered if he could have handled things better and what was going to happen next. After ten years' service he had still not accustomed himself as to how his actions as a policeman could so radically alter the lives of others. Purely as a result of what he saw or didn't see, acted upon or not, they could be incarcerated, executed even – or remain free.

This was not, he realized, a sensible subject of contemplation for a detective police officer. Most of his colleagues merely enjoyed the thrill of the chase and were duly elated when it proved successful, or disappointed when not. At least, that's how it seemed. Maybe that was the right way.

Perhaps his over-sensitivity was self-indulgent and had now led him to make a foolish decision as regards Jessie. Should he have followed the proper procedure, arrested her and let others better equipped decide her fate, rather than send her back to where she could be in great danger?

That was being dramatic, he chastized himself. No reason why they should suspect Jessie, her father being so thick with them. From what he had gathered from Jessie and his own deductions, Berger's involvement with Dawes and Helman was many stranded. He found customers among the servant girls in the big houses, dropped off some of their 'parcels' for them, possibly, Best suspected, among the foundations on the building sites he worked upon.

Then there would be the lucrative business of blackmail, so often associated with this trade, particularly of guilty married males. He might well carry this out alone, being directly involved with the sources, or be in cahoots with Dawes and Helman.

As for Jessie, she'd been brought up in a hard school so might just prove him wrong and appear with just the information he needed, and which could save her bacon into the bargain.

Best was sitting by the fountain in the same, secluded little square where Jessie and he had spoken so seriously after he had caught her depositing the small corpse. A tranquil spot. One of Islington's fast disappearing green oases, it was surprisingly quiet, considering that just through the alleyway between the National Provincial Bank and Miss Andrews Baby Linen Warehouse lay lively Upper Street.

He was early for their meeting on this bright, still, sunny morning. Nursemaids had brought their charges to play on the lawn, but some of the older ones preferred kicking their way through the heaps of gold and brown leaves on the paths or searching for the biggest and shiniest conkers lying beneath the horsechestnut trees.

All in all, it was a pleasant change of scene for Best. He got up and strolled around the long, oval section of lawn, discreetly kicking a few leaves himself, not even caring if some of them clung to his shiny boots. He passed the old well, from which nursemaids guarded the children lest a terrible accident should befall them, and arrived back to where the criss-crossing paths dissected the ground into ornamental plots. This was the end nearest Upper Street and where the occasional weary shopper rested their feet near the pretty fountain, but there was none now. Too early, perhaps.

Best settled back on a seat, took out his cigarettes and match case as he relaxed into a pleasant reverie. No point in expecting Jessie to be on time. She had told him that Mrs

Dawes sent her out on messages every morning after she'd finished her jobs – at about eleven o'clock – therefore, he realized, she could scarcely be precise about the time. It was now twenty-five minutes past eleven.

Jessie had not turned up for their rendezvous but Best was not unduly alarmed. Anything could have happened. Mrs Dawes might have sent someone else on her errands or not needed anything that day, or she could have sent out Lizzie, the drab skivvy, instead. He would return to the square tomorrow morning and, meanwhile, watch out for her in the John Street back garden.

There had been no sign of Jessie in the garden while he had been out, Mrs O'Connor reported, and another girl had hung out the washing. The girl who took it in that afternoon was small and dark, and Best had not seen her before. He began to feel uneasy. Time for that promised return visit to Mrs Dawes. A surprise return visit, this time.

The same, little, dark girl he'd seen earlier came to the door. 'I'll see if Mrs Dawes is in,' she told him as she showed him into the chilly front parlour. He waited for what seemed a long time, chafing his arms and hands to warm them up. When Mrs Dawes finally appeared she was all primped up but could not disguise that unfocused look of someone who had recently been awoken. Ah, yes. Her afternoon nap and possibly a nip of liquid comfort.

'Do excuse the unscheduled call,' he apologized, 'but I felt we were interrupted last time, before you had time to finish our little tour.'

'Oh, Mr Best. You are welcome any time.' She forced a sincere smile. 'Our favourite neighbour!' He sensed a flurry of activity in the background. She reached for her handbell. 'Do let me get you some refreshment.'

'No, no. Really. That's not necessary. I'd be happy just to finish our little tour.'

When they had done so and were sitting back in the now warmer parlour, discussing the promising investment prospects in such an establishment, he said innocently, 'Oh, may I speak to Jessie?'

'Jessie?' Mrs Dawes frowned.

'Yes; I've a little good news for her and her father about the Lord Mayor's Fund payouts and—'

'Oh, I don't think Jessie would understand anything about such things. Much better to speak to her father.'

'Well, maybe I can ask her to let him know I want a word ... '

'No, no, I can do that.'

'Of course, of course. But I would like to see her. I feel that my being acquainted with her poor sister comforts her a little and—'

'She's not here.'

'She's left?'

'Oh, no. She wasn't looking too well, so I gave her the day off.'

That didn't ring true. Mrs Dawes being solicitous of her servants. But if she was telling the truth, Jessie, surely, should be at home? Although suddenly frantic to leave, Best tried to suppress the panic which was starting to grip him so he could bring his visit to a calm and natural end. It wasn't easy.

Jessie wasn't at home. At least, there was no answer to his knock at the house down in Stroud's Vale. Where could they all be?

When Jessie failed to turn up at their meeting point the following morning, he threw caution to the winds and went back next door.

'The little minx has upped and left,' said Mrs Dawes crossly. 'There's gratitude for you!'

Best's heart sank like a stone. He forced himself to give a rueful smile and shake his head at the ingratitude of young people these days before allowing himself to become involved in discussions about what was clearly Mrs Dawes's favourite subject: money – and how much he was prepared to invest.

They were all running like the wind. The man who had been studiously inspecting the drain in the road; the postman, shedding his bag as he went and the four workmen who had been chatting together just along the street – all were speeding towards 7 John Street. They were trying to get there as Best braced himself against the open door and hung on to a struggling Lizzie while keeping his hand over her mouth to stop her raising the alarm. Speed and secrecy were of the essence. But, in his heart of hearts, Best realized it was all too late.

He had tried to look nonchalant and relaxed when, once again, he had knocked on the front of number seven. Once again he was without an appointment, but this time it was just after dawn. Lizzie had answered, looked puzzled, and then terrified as Best had grabbed her while jamming his foot in the door and beckoning to those men now running towards them.

Soon they were all in – even a gasping, wheezing Cheadle disguised in a paint-stained overall and cap. He'd insisted on taking part and Best had scarcely been able to resist, given that it had been made plain that this parlous state of affairs was all down to a certain, newly appointed, detective inspector. Despite Cheadle's dangerously puce colour, Best could tell that the old man was thrilled to be back in the thick of it.

Best kept his hand tightly over Lizzie's mouth as the plain-clothes policemen spread through the house like a swarm of ants – into the front parlour, the kitchen, upstairs to the bedrooms and servants' quarters and, particularly, down into the cellar and out in the garden and the garden sheds.

One by one they returned, shaking their heads. They'd found heaps of baby clothes and one little corpse, but no sign of the missing Jessie. Soon, three heavily pregnant young women, a dishevelled, dressing-gowned Mrs Dawes and three bewildered maid servants were standing in the hall. But still no sign of Jessie – or her body. How had they removed that without being observed? Cut it up and taken it out in pieces? It didn't bear thinking about. He shuddered.

Back at Islington Police Station a vehement, hissing Mrs Dawes would admit to nothing – so had been left to stew for a while in one of the cells.

A dawn visit had also been made on Dr Helman and he, too, was now occupying a cell on the men's side with two drunks for company. While not exactly drunk himself he was still heavily affected by his previous night's imbibing – a circumstance which, Best and Cheadle soon realized, they could use to their advantage. His resistance would be low. Doubtless he already had a pounding headache, even without the added strain of interrogation. And, of course, after he had learned what Mrs Dawes had been saying …

'Babies die during childbirth,' said Helman almost matter-of-factly. He was trying to hold on to a cool, disdainful professionalism but his hands were trembling as he wiped a film of perspiration from his brow with a none-too-clean handkerchief. 'It happens all the time,' he added, 'it's called being stillborn. A natural occurrence.'

They had told him of the body they had found.

'I expect a post-mortem may prove otherwise in this case,' said Best quietly. He had seen the marks on the baby's neck. He waited for the man to disclaim any knowledge of anything untoward. To remind them that he didn't live on the premises so could scarcely be aware of what went on all the time. But he didn't.

Best listed their other evidence, including his catching Jessie in the act of depositing a body. The news clearly disturbed Helman and, once again, Best waited for a disclaimer, but none came. Instead, an excuse.

'You do realize that since all this business about Mrs Waters and the subsequent inspections by the authorities, the organizers of perfectly respectable and law-abiding lying-in establishments and nurseries become nervous when a baby dies. Sometimes they may attempt to dispose of it so as not to draw attention to themselves. Most unfortunate.' He splayed his hands and put his head to one side in a "let's be reasonable manner", 'But understandable, I think.'

That dealt with the body Jessie had dropped. Hangover or no, Helman was not going to be easy to crack.

'Mrs Dawes was doubtless going to send for me to issue a death certificate for the baby you found on her premises.'

That covered the other corpse – unless the post-mortem said otherwise, but with newborn babies it was notoriously difficult to be certain of the cause of death, and Helman would know that.

The man was sitting up a little straighter now and breathing easier. He pulled down his crumpled waistcoat, dusted off traces of pipe ash, stroked down his hair and whiskers into a smoother outline and looked them coolly in the eye. Oh dear.

'Mrs Dawes says you were party to all the baby murders,' said Best bluntly. 'Indeed, she claims you were the driving force.'

Helman flushed, uncertainty creeping into his eyes. Then suddenly his expression switched to a knowing one. He raised one eyebrow and smiled a small smile. 'I don't think so, gentlemen,' he replied.

'She insists that you blackmailed her into it – even demanded she give herself to you to ensure her safety.'

He'd hit home. Helman tried to remain unmoved by this accusation, but Best could see by the hurt in the man's eyes that he was now on the right track. The two were lovers.

'She says it was repulsive to her, but she had no choice, she had to submit. That it was you alone who did the killing and she was too afraid to resist.'

To Best's astonishment tears started into Helman's eyes. He obviously loved the woman!

Best went in for the kill. 'She found your whisky breath disgusting, she says, and your personal habits quite revolting.'

The tears were trickling down Helman's cheeks and soaking his whiskers. It was probably she who had inveigled him into the business, Best realized.

'May God forgive me,' said Helman.

Me, too, thought Best.

In fact, Mrs Dawes was still insisting her innocence and complete lack of knowledge about what Jessie had been up to with her bundle – 'that wicked child, I never trusted her' – and how the other tiny corpse happened to be on the premises.

She also denied any knowledge of the fate of Nella and Jessie, just as Helman had.

'Nella disappeared just after she had had her baby,' Mrs Dawes insisted, 'and like I told you, Jessie left.'

'Left,' snapped Best, 'why would she do that?'

'Because we told her to!' Mrs Dawes spat out. 'We found her spying on us!' She pulled her fur wrap closer around her. They had allowed her to dress before she left and she had chosen a sensible but expensive-looking, black bombazine day dress, but had not forgotten to add a jet brooch and matching ear-rings which now glittered in the dimly lit interview-room as she shook her head angrily. 'I did nothing to her! Nothing! What do you think I am?'

Oh God. Best bent his head down on to his hands,

rubbed his tired eyes and murmured quietly, 'But you told her father what she had done?'

'Of course! We locked her up until he arrived to take her away.'

Best's nails dug deep into his hands. What an idiot he'd been. Idiot! 'I expect he was angry?'

She nodded. 'Of course,' she said again. 'He was furious – he had a lot to lose – he did well out of us.'

Cursing himself, Best shot out of his chair, bashed open the interview-room door and began to run down the corridor, shouting to Smith and two other startled officers to follow him.

The superintendent's pony and trap would take too long to set up so Best dashed out into Upper Street, prepared to run all the way down to Stroud's Vale or commandeer any passing cart but, to his relief and surprise, they found a cab straight away.

A growler was on its weary way home after a night in the West End but the driver dared not refuse police demands that he take them. Best was beside himself with impatience as the driver did his best to coax some speed out of the exhausted horse. He wanted to jump out and run but knew he would tire and take longer in the end. Anyway, it was too late. Much too late.

Despite his distraction he couldn't help noticing that Smith was refusing to meet his eye, had been, in fact, since they'd met again. Did he feel guilty about revealing Best's whereabouts to Helen?

'What's the matter, man?' he asked eventually.

Smith opened his mouth, struggled to get some words out, then closed it again.

'Look, you made a mistake.' He patted his hand. 'As long as you've learned your lesson.'

This seemed to distress Smith more. He hung his head and mumbled, 'I … I … '

'Tell me, man!' exclaimed Best. 'Just tell me!'

'Joseph's dead.'

All the breath seemed to go out of Best's body. He clutched his chest as though it was going to burst.

'Cheadle said I wasn't to say yet but ... '

'How?' Best managed to choke out. 'How!'

'Scarlet fever. When he fell ill, Matilda sent a message to Helen and she was going to try to reach you. But she daren't come herself – so she sent a message to Cheadle. By the time he got it and came back to her, she'd had another one – to say he was dead.' He reached out and put his arm round the now openly sobbing Best.

When they reached Stroud's Vale, Best had pulled himself together – in time to see Jessie coming up the steps, carrying a pail. Her right eye was closed and swollen, her lips cut and her arms black and blue with bruises. Pushing her roughly from behind was her father.

Best was out of the cab and had launched himself at Berger before anyone could stop him. His attack was ferocious and by the time his colleagues had managed to pull him off he had already done considerable damage.

'At least, Jessie's alive,' panted Smith, as he struggled to restrain his senior officer. 'You *did* save her.'

Chapter Twenty-Three

Back at the police station in Upper Street, Wilhelm Berger was still denying that he had killed Nella.

'She vos my daughter! Vy vould I do that?' he asked belligerently.

'That didn't stop you raping her!' grated Best, who had insisted he was now calm enough to interrogate the man. Indeed, he insisted that having come this far he wanted to be in at the finish, needed to be in at the finish. To his surprise, Cheadle had agreed and left him to it while concentrating on the further questioning of Dr Helman. The results, so far, were a cause of great relief, both to him and the department.

Berger shrugged. 'So? A man gets lonely and needs, you know.' He made a thrusting movement with his pelvis and grinned a little, then winced and touched his swollen eye gingerly.

'Anyvay, vy you say rape? She like it.'

This unapologetic declaration put Smith on the alert. He sat up straighter on his seat in the corner of the interview-room and watched Best anxiously. But Berger's attitude merely encouraged the newly promoted inspector to concentrate more on ensuring that this evil man got his just deserts. Nonetheless, beneath the interview-room table, he clenched and unclenched his fists.

'So when did you kill her?' asked Best matter-of-factly, as though that had been established and Berger had confessed – a ploy which could work. Acting as though guilt was already established and not made much of could bring relief to the perpetrator and even deceive them into thinking that you knew more than you did. This, in turn, could encourage them to give up the struggle. Not this time, though.

'I told you. I no kill Nella,' insisted Berger. His eyes began filling with tears. 'Vy vould I do that?' He shrugged again. 'Because she vos having a baby? Zat vos no problem – except she vouldn't be able to look after the other kids.' He shrugged, 'I just send her to Mrs Dawes. It cost me nothing because I do things for them, and Nella, she help out for her keep.'

'She helped out even when she was long overdue … ' Best paused. 'And that made you angry, didn't it?'

Berger raised his eyebrows wonderingly and shrugged. 'Vy vould it?'

'Because Mrs Dawes was getting impatient and you wanted Nella back home to look after the other kids, and – who knows what else?'

'You make me sound like monster. I not a monster.'

Best realized that he couldn't expect the man to feel guilty about father/daughter incest, it being such a common practice despite never being referred to in polite circles. Or, come to that, any circles. Perhaps that's why it flourished?

'But you beat her when the baby wouldn't come!' he shouted angrily, causing Smith, who had begun to relax again while taking notes, to sit up smartly and even give a discreet little cough. Berger didn't trouble to deny it, merely pursed his lips and put his head on one side in a nodding kind of admission. 'She make me angry, talking about vot happened to the babies … she vouldn't stop.' He spread his hands expressively. 'A father is allowed to—'

'So you were worried she would start to talk? That's why.'

'No!' objected Bergen. 'Vy that vorry me? I go vork for someone else. Not my problem. This baby business, it goes on all the time, everywhere.'

He was right again. And this wasn't getting them anywhere, thought Best. Maybe they should put him back in the cells for a while. Let him stew and see what might bubble to the surface. But frighten him a bit first. Give himself something to contemplate. 'People have been hanged for what you call "this baby business",' Best rammed home. 'And that includes those who aid and abet! The authorities are determined to do something about it. Make an example, like they did with Mrs Waters. Just think about that!'

'It was him! He made me do it!' exclaimed Mrs Dawes, tearfully, when she learned that Helman had told them everything. She was shrewd enough to realize there was no longer any point in denying the known facts – just their interpretation.

'Really? And how did he manage that?' asked Best drily.

'He set a trap. An evil trap!'

Best and Cheadle waited patiently for her to elaborate.

'A baby was born dead. Like babies sometimes are,' she went on. 'These things happen, in the best of lying-in houses,' she added defiantly.

They said nothing, just waited. They knew that there are those who can't bear silence, and judged she might be one of them. Their desire to fill it could sometimes result in careless and gratifying revelations.

She glanced from one to the other, momentarily disconcerted by their lack of response.

'He refused to certify the death!' she exclaimed suddenly, causing them to sit up in surprise, an obviously desired effect to judge by her satisfied expression. 'He threatened to accuse me of killing it – if I didn't help him in this terrible business!' A choking sob escaped her throat and she dabbed bravely at her eyes. 'I was so frightened. A woman on her own. No one to turn to … He told me how Mrs Waters had died. Said he knew the doctor present, how she choked and choked … ' She began acting out the infamous baby-farmer's supposed demise. Suddenly it all became too much for her and she collapsed – somewhat carefully.

Too much for Best as well. Once she had 'recovered', he listened in awe as Mrs Dawes went on to do exactly what he had told Helman she had already done – blame him for everything. She even included the forcible submission to his sexual desires and how repellent that had been to a sensitive woman such as herself.

I'll bet, thought Best. No matter, with Helman's full confession and the other evidence, they had more than enough to charge them both. It was up to the jury to decide whether they believed her version of events. Jessie's evidence should help bring her down and, thank goodness, it would save the girl herself from any charge when she turned Queen's Evidence.

The mystery of Nella's death remained. Neither Helman nor Mrs Dawes would admit to any knowledge of it, which was hardly surprising. They were in enough trouble. As far as they knew she had just left and gone home, they insisted.

A uniformed constable put his head around the door. 'Inspector Best,' he whispered apologetically, 'there's a lady here to see you. She says it's important.'

For once Mrs O'Connor didn't say anything. Her natural ebullience seemed to have faded away. She looked sad, defeated and somehow older as she handed Best a folded piece of lined blue paper.

The message on it was painstakingly penned in black ink and written in a large, angular hand. It read:

To whom it may concern.
I killed Nella. She was going to tell on them and they would have hanged Martha and I loved her. I am sorry. Tell her father and her sister I am sorry. I will go to hell now.
    Robert B. Murphy

'He was down in the cellar,' said Mrs O'Connor. 'Mary found him when she went for the coal. He must have been hanging there all night, poor soul.' She shook her head slowly from side to side.

Best was staggered. He ought to have been alerted by Murphy's outburst about Nella. Had been, in fact, except he had dismissed the idea as being too unlikely. Murphy was just not the sort of man to do such a thing. So much for his having 'a nose' about people. He had no doubt now that the man had reacted impulsively, as he had when he struck out down at North Woolwich. Not knowing what else to do.

'Could that be why he began insisting on getting the coal – saying it was too heavy for the girls to carry?' she asked.

'The body was down there,' nodded Best. He grimaced ruefully. 'Right under my very nose.'

'Now look here, Mr Best, don't you be hugging all the blame to yourself like that,' said Mrs O'Connor. 'Others will be demanding their fair share too. Right under all our noses, I'd say.'

'But how did he get her body to Beckton?' asked Best. He realized as he spoke and held up his hand, 'No, don't tell me … '

They said it in unison.

'Patrick's cart.'

'And wasn't Murphy always bringing back bits and pieces from this house-clearing. Then taking them away again when he'd made them all new again.'

Best nodded. 'What difference would one more large parcel or roll of carpet make? Who'd notice?'

They sat together contemplating the sad end of both Nella and Murphy, and how Nella needn't have died had Murphy known that Martha was to perish soon. It was all too ironic and pathetic – and was probably what made him finally crack and hang himself. Finally, Mrs O'Connor sat up, took a deep breath and said, 'So now I'm to lose my favourite lodger as well?'

'I'll be visiting,' he assured her, grasping her hands. 'Won't be able to survive too long without some of your wonderful dumplings.'

'Mind you do,' she said. 'Bring that lady friend of yours as well, and' – she finished hopefully – 'your wee ones as they arrive.'

'I will, I will,' he promised, equally hopefully.

'Children catch infectious diseases,' said Helen, gripping the arms of her chair. 'You know that.'

Best did, only too well. His young sister Katie had died of measles and his little brother Harry had almost succumbed to diphtheria.

'But he wouldn't have got it if you hadn't sent him away!' he raged. Joseph had caught scarlet fever from little Edward, his best friend. Edward had survived.

'You proposed to keep Joseph away from other children indefinitely?'

'He was weak after the accident and still pining for his mother.'

'All the more reason he should go to Matilda's. He was happy there,' she insisted. 'He was getting better every day just being with those other children. You should have seen him last time … '

Best brushed her words away with a violent gesture. 'I never will now, will I?' he exclaimed. 'I never will!'

He knew he was being unreasonable, holding her responsible for life's injustices. But he couldn't help himself.

She sat impassively for a moment, then said quietly, 'He was very fond of you *but you weren't here.*'

There was a tap on the door.

'Come in, my dear,' said Helen.

A girl entered, carrying a tea tray. A young girl about five months pregnant. 'Hello, Mr Best!' she exclaimed, enjoying his astonishment.

'Hello Jessie,' he replied, pulling himself together suffi-
ciently to smile at her. 'This is a nice surprise!'

She grinned, pleased with herself. She put the tray
down carefully, then began to serve them with great
concentration but much rattling of cups and saucers. She
already looked so much happier and healthier. The bruises
were fading and the lips almost healed.

'Mrs Briggs will be retiring soon and Jessie is taking her
place,' said Helen when Jessie had gone.

Best cleared his throat. 'And what about her baby?'

'Oh, she'll keep it here,' said Helen nonchalantly. 'It was
the least I could do.'

So this child could stay but Joseph couldn't and had died
as a result.

'She's a bright girl,' Helen continued unknowingly. 'I'm
going to teach her to read and write – and maybe even
to paint.' Best said nothing, but thought, well at least she's
softened that much. But it was no good, it wasn't enough.

'Another thing,' said Helen, smiling slightly, her
head coquettishly on one side. 'I think it's time we got
married, don't you? Jessie is young enough to help with
any children and—'

'Go to h—' Best stopped himself and got to his feet.
She was frowning now and gazing up at him quizzically.
'I don't think so,' he said, looking her straight in the eye
before adding quietly, 'it's too late.'

He turned and walked out.

When he reached the pavement outside, he noticed
with a sort of pleasure how the low, wintry sun was
glancing cheerfully off the windows opposite – and he
felt the pronounced nip in the air. He should have worn
his overcoat. Never mind. He smiled to himself. He was
going back to work with his colleagues but at a higher
rank, which meant new responsibilities an d challenges.
It was time to start anew in other ways. His old optimism

was returning. Life was going to get better. He was free and it felt good.

When he reached the corner he tried to resist looking back at the house, but couldn't help himself. She had always stood at the window to wave him off, but this time she wasn't there.

POSTSCRIPT

On 14 November 1878, the Coroner's Jury at the inquest on the collision between the *Princess Alice* and the *Bywell Castle*, found that William Beachey, a stockbroker's clerk, aged 46 years, and others, had died of drowning after the collision – which had not been wilful. His being the first body to be recovered, he represented the 640 'others' now believed lost, although the final figure was never established. Four bodies had been found naked, in an advanced state of putrefaction and in mysterious circumstances. Theirs was a mystery which was never solved.

As for who was to blame for the accident – opinions differed. The inquest jury thought the *Bywell Castle* largely responsible for not easing, stopping and reversing her engines in time but felt that the *Princess Alice* contributed by not going astern and stopping. She also carried more passengers than was prudent.

The Board of Trade Enquiry and Court of Admiralty both put the blame on the *Princess Alice* who should have ported her helm on seeing the other vessel. Further, she had been navigated in a careless and reckless manner but, they felt, the numbers she carried were not excessive for such a craft.

All agreed, however, on the inadequacy of the life-saving equipment on board the pleasure craft but found that, despite accusations to the contrary, the boat was *not* too lightly constructed for her purpose. Indeed, one expert declared that even the *Great Eastern*, the heaviest iron merchant ship then in existence, could not have withstood the impact.

Attention was also drawn to the lack of navigational discipline among Thames traffic, the disgusting state of the water at the impact site, and the fact that loss of life would have been less had the boat not sank so quickly and more passengers been able to swim.

Three days after the last of these findings came the death of the woman after whom the ill-fated pleasure steamer had been named. Princess Alice was Queen Victoria's second daughter and wife of the Grand Duke of Hesse-Darmstadt. All of her six children had caught diphtheria and one of them, Princess Mary, had died in consequence.

Fearing the loss of her only son, Ernest, the princess kissed and comforted him – and contracted the disease herself. She succumbed on 14 December – the same date that her father, Prince Albert, had passed away seventeen years earlier. The other children survived. One of these, Princess Victoria, named her daughter Alice. She was to become the mother of Prince Philip, the Duke of Edinburgh.

Queen Victoria was devastated by Princess Alice's death but thought it 'almost incredible and most mysterious' that the loving daughter had been 'called back' on that particular day to the father she had tended on his deathbed.

14

Visit our website and discover thousands of other
History Press books.

www.thehistorypress.co.uk